*»I am you. My origin is by chance.
My future uncertain.«*

Bibliographic Information of the German National Library:
The German National Library lists this publication in the German National Bibliography. Detailed bibliographic data is available on the Internet at http://dnb.dnb.de.

Automated analysis of this work to extract information—especially regarding patterns, trends, and correlations—according to §44b of the German Copyright Act (UrhG) ("text and data mining") is prohibited.

© 2025 Marty Karbassion
Editing: Marty Karbassion
Proofreading: Marty Karbassion
Additional Contributors: Marty Karbassion
Publisher: BoD · Books on Demand GmbH, Überseering 33, 22297 Hamburg, bod@bod.de
Printing: Libri Plureos GmbH, Friedensallee 273, 22763 Hamburg
ISBN: 978-3-8192-6612-6

WAR
IN OUR
Hearts

THE SCENT
OF A BURNED
FUTURE

Table of Contents

A Journey into the Unknown

It can't be true, I keep telling myself that this is all just a dream. Frightened, I stare at the ground, and with every wave crashing against the hull of our boat on this starry night, I realize that I've left behind the most precious thing in the world. Panic-stricken, I reach into the inner pocket of my jacket and pull out a family photo, which I gaze at with a sigh. There he is, my whole pride! And here they all are united again. On the far left is my delicate mom, Fadia, looking into the camera with her ominous smile, as if she had already sensed what awaited us in the near future. Next to her stands my father, Karim, who with his gray mustache and sturdy posture resembles an aging soldier about to go off to war. Right beside him, you can see my uncle, sporting an impenetrable expression as the photographer captures us. As I looked up again, the frightened faces of several older men and some women, holding their children protectively in their arms, immediately caught my eye. Silence reigns among us, and the only sound I hear is the grinding noise of our outboard motor, laboring through the restless sea. What has become of my country? How did it come to this? These thoughts incessantly whirl in my mind until I gather the courage to turn back once more. Shocked, I look up at the brightly lit salvos of rockets reflecting on the water's surface, hurtling down with lightning speed towards my homeland, my future, and my fellow countrymen. Over there in the distance was where I wanted to spend my life, amidst my grandfather's date palms, among

3

the many ancient ruins that the past had left us with its beautiful stories. One thought follows another until someone suddenly speaks to me from the side. The face of the old man, weathered by life, and before I sink back into my sorrow, he says something that would stay with me forever on this journey.

»Look, it's not the enemy attacking us, but we are attacking ourselves.« he pointed at the explosions. I was initially frozen and didn't quite know how to respond, when suddenly a conversation with my grandfather came to mind, one we had during a walk together some time ago.

»Diyar, my boy, look at this beautiful nature surrounding us. Everything on this earth is transient. The plants over there, the eagle above us, and the tree, which with its many branches tells us about its life. Just yesterday, it was full of leaves, and today, it is bare and dried out.«

»But Grandpa, life seems so endless, as if it will never fade away.«

»You think that because you're still young and life seems eternal to you. Look at the tree as a whole. What does it signify to you?«

»Mmmh, it's towering and proudly swaying in the wind.«

»Oh, I love how you see the world. Come, try again, and this time, focus on each individual vibration it sends to you.« Diyar was obviously contemplating, nervously biting his lip before responding.

»Well, it's just there and doesn't bother any-one.«

»Yes, that's not too far off.«

»Well, unlike this tree, we humans somehow always get in our own way, don't you think?«

»That's quite true, but have you ever thought about why that is?«

»Well, I don't understand why we can't peacefully coexist. Back when I was very young and played with kids from the neighborhood, everything seemed possible without conflicts.«

»Fantastic, I sense you know exactly what I'm getting at. Would you like to discuss it or shall I explain?«

»No, go ahead. You know how much I enjoy listening to you. Besides, no one understands the world as well as you do.« he replied with a smile.

»Okay, but do me the favor of sitting there in the shade, I'm melting in this heat.«

»Alright, go ahead and tell me now.«

Bennou accepted his grandson's impatience with a smile, settling down on the ground. He leisurely tugged at his white full beard several times before continuing.

»Children come into this world without knowledge, relying solely on instinct. At a certain age, they consciously perceive their surroundings and absorb the behaviors and mindsets of their parents like a sponge. They are influenced in decisions about what they eat, with whom they play, and whom they avoid. The problem, however, lies in the fact that their own life experiences shape their upbringing, which can be both negative and positive. Do you understand this so far?«

»Of course, I may be young, but I'm not foolish.«

»Children grow into adults throughout life.

In this lengthy process, they accumulate their own experiences, which they integrate into society through their words and actions. However, many of them maintain or develop a limited perspective, and therein lies the problem.«

»But why?« he asked, curious.

»A person who doesn't think freely is dangerous because they can be manipulated by those to whom they are useful.«

»Hold on, wait a moment, I need to process this first. So, it means that people go through life with a predetermined perspective from the start and some are more easily influenced by it, especially those whose thinking isn't free. But I don't understand why anyone would manipulate people? Everyone can think what they want!«

»Certainly, everyone is entitled to their own

thoughts. However, the problem lies in the fact that our thinking determines our actions, and that's where politicians come into play. The reason they hold so much power in our country or in other countries is that there are individuals who share their views. But if the majority of the people were more skeptical and questioned everything logically happening around them, it would look very different. Let's say you're hungry. Would you eat everything given to you?«

»Of course! I'd happily fill my stomach.«

»You see, those people who strive for change and possess little or nothing are made dependent on politics. Because they act out of sheer desperation and end up standing for or fighting for something that didn't originate from their worldview or idea. That can be racial hatred or another pathological ideology that sooner or later ends in total chaos. The reason why you were able to play peacefully and without problems with the neighborhood children back then is quite simply due to lack of influence. You and your little friends were free in your thinking and acted on instinct. It never occurred to you to exclude someone because they looked different or belonged to a different social class. Your toys back then were paper airplanes and sandcastles. The toys of politicians and adults today are power and status. They all bear responsibility for the misery in the world because they wage war. War within their hearts.« Before he could finish his next thought, he was abruptly jostled by the older gentleman, who brought him back to the present with a »Hey, are you daydreaming?«

»No, I'm not. But I just don't know what to

answer. Why would we attack ourselves? It just doesn't make sense.« he underscored, shrugging his shoulders.

»I didn't expect anything else from a greenhorn like you. But let me explain. The weapons turning our country into rubble and ashes in the distance, they're from us.«

»How, from us? We're being attacked by another country right now. How can they be from us then?«

»Everything in life has a cycle. If I cause suffering to your family, then one day you'll come looking for me and, most likely, seek revenge. Isn't that right?«

»Probably, yes.«

»For decades, our politics have supplied weapons to countries all over the world, deliberately inciting peoples against each other and thus creating blazing conflict zones. They didn't care at all about who gets hold of the tools of the devil—dictators, kings, and other despots. They just carried on, knowing that their actions would eventually come back to haunt them. The sad part is, people mean nothing to them because in our society, numbers matter more than every broken heart that desperately calls out for its mother.« Diyar nodded in understanding, listening attentively.

»Just look around. Everyone on this rickety boat is dirt poor and only has what they're wearing. It's us who have to flee, not the politicians or the elite who escape abroad with their deceitful talk and their ill-gotten wealth. I've left my life behind and lost everything, my two sons, my wife, and my future. At first, I was a follower of their lies because I hoped for a better future for myself and my family. But then, it was too late, and eventually, their false promises and greed for power led these tyrants to take away everything my people and I loved. You should be glad you got out of hell in time, my children weren't as lucky as you.«

»I'm terribly sorry, but without my father's good connections, I would have never made it onto this boat.« The old man looked over angrily and curiously inquired about the boy's parents.

»Do your parents hold an important position in the country or are they part of the party? If so, then I'd shut up right away, I don't have much respect for those bastards.«

»No, neither. But I can't help that I ended up here. I'm the only child in our family.«

»Your statement fills me with blind rage.

Not only are you the only child, but you're also the only boy who stands out to me immediately. Do you think it's fair while back home, young men like you are defending their families?« Diyar sought help from the woman beside him, who stepped in protectively.

»Leave the boy alone right now, or you'll have to deal with me.« The old man turned away in offense, discreetly eavesdropping on their introduction.

»Sorry for butting in, but I couldn't stand the drivel from the old geezer anymore. By the way, my name is Zainab, and the little one next to me is my son, Adil.« Diyar looked gratefully and gently caressed the little one's face when suddenly the boat's outboard motor, billowing smoke, gave up its service. An alarmed sigh swept through the rows, and all eyes turned to the poor man. He cursed as he removed the plastic covering of the engine and armed himself with a flashlight to search for the problem. In their desperation, everyone huddled closer and began to whisper. Shortly after, a gray-haired man pointed at Diyar, who was meticulously questioned about the story of his escape.

The Scent of a Burned Future

I still vividly remember the scent that lingered in my memories every morning as I left the house. The air was filled with the aroma of sweet pastries, slowly melding with all the other scents as I ventured further into the city. On my way to school, I passed by a fruit vendor who arranged his goods at sunrise, cheerfully whistling his favorite tune. Baba called him Mr. Impeccable because he meticulously cleaned each piece of fruit with a brush before displaying them. Whenever I bought from him, he'd share a philosophical anecdote that, as a child, I pondered incessantly but never truly understood. One of them, however, has become etched in my mind and now makes sense amidst this atrocious war.

»We're all on a journey through life. A life that can be remarkably beautiful for those who stand on the right side.« Everyone on board immediately felt connected and encouraged Diyar, who had to pause briefly before continuing. My best friend Nabih always waited for me on the way to school at the main road. As soon as he spotted me through his round glasses, he'd enthusiastically wave and chatter away like a waterfall, even though he could see I could barely keep my eyes open from fatigue. Every time, we took a detour, passing by a magnificent river into a park adorned with colorful flowers and splendid date palms. There, we talked about things we still wanted to experience and planned the countries we wanted to visit together. Nabih was fascinated by ancient Egypt, a topic his knowledge could fill an encyclopedia with. Initially, I was enamored with dinosaurs, but over time, his passion fueled mine so intensely that I completely forgot about the giant reptiles, eagerly anticipating boarding that airplane that would catapult us like time travelers into the land of the Pharaohs. During our conversations, we fantasized endlessly, creating colossal castles in the air without boundaries. At times, Nabih was so consumed by his imagination that we'd spend our free time together in the desert, digging massive holes, pretending to be on an excavation. With every bone or shard of pottery we found, Nabih would cheerfully thrust the spade into the air, shouting so loudly toward the blue sky that even Cleopatra herself could have heard him. It was terribly embarrassing for me, but the older we got, the more I let my enthusiasm run wild.

»Imagine if, on our next expeditions, we discovered a skull or an ancient tomb. Then we'd be rich and famous overnight.« he beamed from ear to ear.

»And I foolishly thought I was the bigger dreamer of the two of us.«

»It was clear from the start that you weren't, Nabih. You can't even hide your emotions from an old brick. Let's just say we actually found something. You'd have a desert collapse immediately.«

»You can say that again. If archaeologists dig me up two thousand years later, at least I'd be a saint.«

»Don't talk nonsense. They'd instantly know you're a pauper just by looking at your clothes.«

»You think so? How would they know? This fine fellow here looks like the picture of health.« he bragged, running his hand through his hair.

»Yeah, for now. In a millennium, your black curly head will look like a shriveled raisin, and your decaying body will smell like a damned mummy. Besides, there won't be any gold or other treasures in your tomb. I know that much about you. Funny how you act as if you don't know. The only things we can call our possessions are our families, and that can't be weighed in gold.«

»I fully agree with you. By the way, I wanted to ask you last time if you've been to Monsieur Friedrich's yet?«

»You never let it go, do you? Do you really

believe that old shard with those strange hiero-glyphs we found years ago has any value? Think about it. There have probably never been people in this desert besides us. That thing probably fell from the sky and got buried in the ground during the first monsoon.«

»You know, presuming isn't knowing. So, do me a favor and still go see the old German guy as soon as possible. I would do it myself, but he hasn't forgotten about that Nazi thing. By the way, there's something else that's been bothering me.«

»Come on, spill it. I consider that Nazi thing just as much a tall tale as the one-legged beggar who supposedly chased you at night, wanting to beat the life out of you for no rea-son.«

»I admit, the beggar story was a bit far-fetched. But you can tell me whatever you want, behind the blue eyes of this Friedrich lies something ice-cold. So, be careful when you're with him. Don't believe everything, he wouldn't hesitate to do even the unthinkable.«

»Has your dad spoken to his contact yet? With the war escalating so rapidly, I fear it might engulf us like an avalanche, and we won't get out of hell in time. Yesterday, the newspaper claimed our military is the strongest in the world and could stand up to anyone. But who, in their right mind, believes that? Our tanks are ready for the museum, and our planes are so covered in sand that even the desert would envy them. The Europeans are steering clear of us and won't meddle in this conflict because there's nothing to gain here except a few spices.«

»It's not that simple. Baba hasn't found the right opportunity to meet his contact yet. Dangers are lurking everywhere, and nobody trusts anyone anymore, afraid of ending up in prison. I'll let you know as soon as I have more information, but it might take a while.« Diyar looked over questioningly at his friend, who raced up a sand dune and excitedly signaled for him to come closer.

»We don't have much time left. Look out for those dark smoke clouds in the distance and take a deep breath. Do you smell that?«

»Yes, it smells like something burning.«

»My mom told me yesterday, it's not just a scent. That's the scent of a burnt future. If we don't want to get caught in the crossfire, we need to come up with something quick.«

Seconds later, he was jolted from his thoughts

as the boat's engine roared in the background, only to fall silent soon after. Once the disappointment faded from their faces, all eyes turned back to Diyar, who continued in a subdued tone. Two weeks later, I was in town with my father, Karim. You could sense something was up because people were behaving differently than usual. Whenever we tried to make eye contact, they turned away or looked straight through us. Many shops were closed or looked like they'd been plundered overnight. Even Mian, my barber, who usually worked like a maniac seven days a week, left his customers standing with a 'closed today' sign on the door. Dad seemed very nervous that day. I could tell from his stony expression and the quick pace I could barely keep up with. He didn't tell me where we were going, which was unusual because he never kept things from me. Yet, I bombarded him with questions that went unanswered until we stopped in front of an inconspicuous hotel near the harbor. Without hesitation, I followed my father. He met a shady-looking man with sunglasses in a dark corner of the lobby, handing him an envelope silently before disappearing. On our way back, we settled on a sandbag, which had become a common sight throughout the city for protection against attacks. Baba had always been someone who had a grip on the situation and his emotions. But on that day, he sat before me like a broken man, crying bitterly. I hugged him as tightly as I could, feeling the tears streaming down his cheeks, tears of helplessness. When he somewhat composed himself, he looked up at me and spoke so softly that I could barely understand him.

»Diyar, my son, we'll have to part ways for an indefinite time.« Frozen, I looked over, feeling my heart shatter into pieces and trying desperately to gather the fragments. Fear surged within me, and despite already knowing the outcome of the conversation, I asked the question anyway.

»Baba, what's going on? What are you hiding from me?«

»In less than two weeks, you'll board a boat at the harbor that will take you away from here. I'm terribly sorry. I meant to tell you much earlier, but I just didn't have the courage. Now, I'm sitting here, looking into the eyes of my child, and this endless weight that I've been carrying for months overwhelms me again.«

»But why? Everything seems fine.«

»Please don't be naive. Can't you feel it? The restlessness creeping in slowly, replacing joy in life. That's not a good sign. The war has escalated dramatically in recent weeks. The western countries are supplying the invaders with massive amounts of weapons, and we have nothing to counter. It's only a matter of a few weeks before we're overrun.«

»Do you really believe it'll happen exactly like that? Have you talked to Bennou about it?«

»Bennou, Bennou, all I hear is Bennou. Your grandpa wants to explain everything with his sharp mind and life lessons. But with these people, that doesn't exist. The only language they speak is violence. I don't care how it'll end, but I'll never allow my only son to fall into their hands. Do you understand?« Desperation was written all over Diyar's face, causing him to take a few seconds before a hesitant »Yes« escaped his lips.

»Don't look so sad. We have to adapt to the situation and act quickly. Trust me, better days will come. Come on, let's slowly head back home so that Mum Fadia doesn't worry.« As they walked through the dusty streets, Diyar couldn't stop thinking about Nabih, who was stuck in his mind. He fervently prayed that the old shard had some value so he could get his beloved friend to safety in time.

Monsieur Friedrich

Early in the morning, he grabbed the artifact from his excavation and headed towards Monsieur Friedrich. Just before reaching his destination, he changed direction and paid a visit to his grandpa, who was taking a stroll on his date plantation. Shouting loudly, Diyar ran towards him, causing Bennou to turn around in surprise.

»What are you doing here so early, and why are you crowing as if your life depends on it?« Bennou asked. Completely out of breath, Diyar mumbled to himself, initially causing confusion as his counterpart could only grasp fragments.

»Wait, wait. Before you continue, take a deep breath first I didn't understand anything except 'envelope, Bennou said.

»Phew, okay, he breathed several times.

»Yesterday, I was with Baba in a hotel down at the harbor. There, he handed an envelope to a strange guy with sunglasses. Afterwards, he told me that soon I'll be boarding a boat to get away from here because the war is getting closer. Did you know about this?« Bennou seemed visibly surprised and took a moment to contemplate before responding.

»No, your father didn't utter a single word about it. That's extremely strange because he usually discusses everything with me. Can you still remember the sentence I gave you in our last conversation?«

»Of course, I remember, but what does that have to do with the situation?«

»Much more than you think. If you don't

understand this thought construct, your life will always consist of good and evil because you seek the causes of chaos in the world on the surface and not within yourself. Even if it's challenging for you right now, repeat what stuck with you from our last conversation.« Reluctantly, Diyar reflected inwardly, and although he wasn't in the mood for contemplation, he tried to articulate everything as best as he could.

»Well, you said that as children, we acted on instinct and were thus free in our thinking because there was no external influence. Our toys were paper planes and sandcastles. The toys of politicians and adults are status and power. Everyone is responsible for the misery in the world because they carry war in their hearts. But what exactly do you mean by that?«

»Very good, Diyar. I'm amazed how well you can listen. Let's say you're in a terribly bad mood and you're meeting one of your friends. On the way there, you're having an internal conflict. If you don't pull yourself together now, you'll inevitably take out what you're feeling inside on those around you. Are you following me so far?«

»Mmmh, yeah. But what does that have to do with the war in our hearts?«

»Have patience, have patience. The external conflict that exists always precedes a conflict that once took place within ourselves. A small conflict, like the one that occurs in you or me, will have no major consequences. But a conflict that occurs in a person who holds a lot of power and responsibility can plunge the world into the abyss. However, no matter how big or small the conflict may be, you must analyze it with an alert mind. So that it dissolves through direct understanding and does not build up into something big that eventually takes root and leads to war in your heart.« With a thoughtful expression, Diyar absorbed what was said and spoke right after.

»Grandpa, is it okay if we discuss this another time? Right now, I have completely different worries. I am torn inside, and honestly, I am terribly afraid. What would you do in my place? Should I listen to Baba and leave my home and you, or should I wait until the army is at our doorstep?« Bennou pondered for a while, observing his grandson, who paced nervously and contemplatively looked at the red-orange shimmering piece of pottery in his hand.

»If I were you, I would listen to your father, ultimately, he bears the responsibility for his family, so my opinion is entirely irrelevant. What have you been holding in your hand all this time? Show me.«

Bennou looked down with interest at the artifact, a questioning "Hmmm" escaping his lips.

»My goodness, don't make it so suspenseful. Tell me if this thing is real, I haven't slept a wink all night.«

»I can't tell you that, but even if it is, you're not allowed to keep it. You have to return it to the country it belongs to. Where did you get it, and why are you carrying it around?«

»I've owned it for a few years, Nabih and I found it during our previous excavations. A few kilometers outside the city, near the old military base where you were once stationed.

What if someone stole it, and it belongs to no one? Can I then consider it my property?«

»Why are you suddenly acting so peculiar, and why is this thing so important to you? Come on, spill it.« Diyar hemmed and hawed incessantly before finally coming clean.

»Well, I wanted to sell it and use the money to help my best friend so that he can join me on this boat because I'm afraid he won't make it in time otherwise.«

»You have ideas. And where or to whom were you planning to sell it? The first street vendor who crosses your path?« Bennou gave his grandson a tap on the back of his head.

»Well, Monsieur Friedrich, he knows about these things.« Diyar replied. Bennou stared over in shock, took a moment to gather himself before finding the right words.

»That old Friedrich, that strange hermit, no one knows where he comes from or what he did in his former life. Some say he fought for the Nazis in the war and showed no mercy to his enemies. Others say he didn't fire a single shot and preferred the loss of his comrades to the death of an innocent person. Even if the truth probably lies somewhere in between, I would advise you not to get involved with him, as you never know what to expect.«

»I understand what you mean, but he's the only one who knows about artifacts like this. Besides, didn't you always say that a person should be judged by their deeds? So, if we don't know what he did in the past, we can't condemn him, right?«

»I must agree with you there. But do me a favor and be cautious when you talk to him.

Don't let yourself be taken advantage of, and refuse any trade in any case. Now, get going, I have a lot of work ahead of me. But you're welcome to stay and help me with the date harvest. I could use all the assistance I can get.« Diyar politely declined and headed quickly to his original destination. Along the bustling streets, he was overcome by a strange feeling that didn't leave him until someone tapped him on the shoulder from behind. It was Nabih, who grinned widely and winked at him, momentarily leaving Diyar speechless.

»Good Lord, do you always have to sneak up like that? Someday it'll backfire, I'm telling you. Besides, I almost dropped the pottery. That would have been the end, and we could have picked up the shards of hope together.

How long have you been trailing me?« Diyar exclaimed.

»Good grief, your mood is so gloomy that even the god of good vibes would avoid you. I've been observing you since you were at Bennou's. From a distance, your mood see med relatively normal, though.« Nabih replied.

»Don't act so high and mighty. My mood isn't that bad. By the way, Grandpa couldn't really say much about our find. But with old Friedrich, he has a divided opinion, which honestly didn't really help me. It's actually good that you're here, you can keep watch and get help if anything happens.«

»Great, I get to do the dirty work again while you deal with life's important matters. It's like ancient Egypt all over again. There, slaves had to drag monstrous stones in scorching heat until their legs gave out.« Nabih symbolically dropped to the sand.

»You can still walk, you old storyteller, and you don't look that exhausted, so pipe down. The biggest risk, by the way, will stick to me. Because if the German decides to strangle me for some reason, you'll just stand there daydreaming and won't notice a thing because you're always mentally elsewhere.«

»You can be really mean, you know that?«

»Well, of course. With you, it's especially fun because you always look so bewildered. Look, his shop is over there. Just stay here and act normal, I don't want us to attract unnecessary attention.« Nabih exaggerated the situation and then playfully formed a triangle with his hands above his head, resembling a pyramid while his friend laughing crossed the street. Upon arriving there, he entered the dimly lit shop, immediately encountering the musty smell emanating from the numerous books stacked in shelves all around. Carefully navigating through a narrow aisle past a few ancient vases, he inadvertently brushed against the keys of an antique piano, producing a melodious sound that summoned the owner. With wide eyes, he looked over to the giant who marched towards him, asking about his intentions in German-accented English. Mouth agape, Diyar stared up into the cold blue eyes. A series of horror scenarios raced through his mind, transforming into pure fear as Monsieur Friedrich began cursing in his native language. Without thinking, he dashed outside, where Nabih followed the dust cloud, ending in a nearby alley. There, Diyar leaned against a building, gasping for air and clutching his heart, which was pounding wildly from the fright.

»Hey, either you just made the fastest deal of your life or feared for it. I'd prefer the former. But judging by the big beads of sweat on your forehead, I think you pulled the scaredy-cat move.« Nabih remarked.

»Man, you know everything. Believe me, if you had looked into Grandpa's murky eyes, you would have shot like a rocket headfirst through the window.« Diyar replied.

»Haha, those are just assumptions. In our first encounter, I called him a Nazi right away and walked proudly out of his shop.«

»You dreamer! Sounds more like you're riding camels in the desert.« Diyar mimicked the motion.

»Now take it easy. If we keep debating here forever, we'll never know if that weird thing is genuine. So, what's the plan?« Diyar sighed with a wink, panic creeping into his pockets, which Nabih naturally noticed.

»Please, don't tell me you lost the pottery now.«

»Damn, I think I left it in the store.«

»This can't be serious. You know what that means, right?«

»Yeah, we have to go back immediately and ask if Friedrich will give it back to us.« Diyar determinedly declared.

»Fine and dandy, Mr. Know-it-all. And how were you planning to prove to him that the shard belongs to you? You coward, you didn't even show it to him. We'll do this my way. We wait until after sunset, break into his shop, and get it back. But first, we need to figure out where the thing is. Come on, let's get started, I don't want to linger here forever.« In a brisk pace, they made their way back to the store, positioning themselves inconspicuously by a window.

»And Diyar, can you see anything?«

»Yes.«

»And what?«

»Your hair, your noggin is blocking the entire window.«

»Man, I'm sorry, but...«

»Quiet, something's happening.« At that moment, the owner passed by the piano, where the red-orange pottery shard lay. He picked it up, looking puzzled. The two visibly sighed with relief, only to startle when old Friedrich tucked the artifact into his shirt pocket.

»Oh holy moly, your plan totally back-fired.«

»Why, let me see.«

»Why? Because the old fool pocketed our object of desire. Now we need to act quickly, and I already have an idea.« Diyar put on a sly grin, immediately interrupted by his friend, who excitedly interjected.

»I got it! You want to kill him and bury him in the desert afterward.«

»What's wrong with you? Nobody wants to off anybody.«

»Ah, I see. So, you want to make it look like an accident. Very clever!«

»You fool, that would be the same thing, just without getting our hands dirty. No, we'll wait until he leaves the shop and then follow him.«

»Well great, that's a brilliant plan. I found my suggestion much more creative.«

»I wasn't finished, genius. Afterward, we'll intentionally bump into him on the street, and you'll subtly reach into his shirt pocket. Any questions?«

»Yes, quite a few. Why do I have to do the grunt work again? And why don't we just do it my way from the start?«

»Firstly, because those who ask questions are always the ones in line. And secondly, because your absurd fantasies have nothing to do with reality. Is that so hard to understand? Don't ask me any unnecessary counter-questions, or I'll explode in anger.« Nabih sulked silently and avoided starting an unnecessary argument in the following hours. As the afternoon signaled the end of the workday, the old man left his shop precisely on time. The two skillfully blended in with the pedestrians and strolled casually behind him. After almost an hour, they became suspicious. The shadowed figure marched briskly ahead towards the desert, where their pursuit abruptly ended. Hidden behind a rock, the two observed the perplexing scene in the midst of the barren landscape. The old man stopped in front of a few stacked stones and bowed, saying the following: »*My comrades, I miss the time when total strangers became friends. When unity and loyalty were not just words but actions.*«

»Diyar, did you understand anything of what he mumbled?«

»No, how could I? My German isn't the best. What about you?«

»The only German word in my vocabulary

is 'Nazi,' you clown.« Both burst into cheerful laughter, catching Monsieur Friedrich's attention as he turned towards them. The two literally felt their hearts drop, especially evident in Diyar's expression.

»Shh, Nabih, be quiet, he's looking our way.«

»Huh? Why are you getting all worked up? Weren't you the one talking big just now? Come on, now's the chance to go to him and introduce yourself. Meanwhile, you can sneak a grin and grab whatever's in his breast pocket. Nothing can go wrong, my prayers are on your side.«

»With so much sarcasm, it's obvious you come from an artistic family.«

»What are you blabbering about? An artistic family? Baba was a vegetable seller, not in the theater.«

»Oh, it's all the same.«

»You rascal, I'd love to give you a good punch right now.« He raised his fist threateningly.

»People who talk a lot usually don't follow through in the end. Instead, check out good old Friedrich, he just threw our pottery shard into the sand and is heading home again.« Carefully, Nabih peeked out from behind the rock, ready to leave his hiding spot, but his friend prevented it with a firm grip.

»Stay put, you crazy bird.« At that moment, the old man turned around once more before disappearing into the distance. Relieved, they emerged from their hiding place and went over to where their find lay. They looked around questioningly when an idea struck Diyar.

»I know why he was here. This is the place

where his comrades are buried. That's why he bowed. Think logically, people in cemeteries do that too.«

»Nonsense. People who pray bow as well. But you know what's strange?«

»What? Spit it out!«

»Just earlier, in your eyes, I was the one with completely absurd fantasies, and now you're coming up with far-fetched theories that make no sense at all. The stones around here probably just ended up here by chance. But what makes me suspicious is our find. Why did he casually toss it into the desert? It just doesn't make sense.« Nabih puzzled.

»Every time I look at you, I wonder which part of your misshapen egghead collided with which wall. You won't become a scientist in this life for sure. I stick to my claim and say that right here in the sand in front of us lie his dead comrades.«

»Yeah, so what? What does that do for us? Should we dig and check?«

»That's right. No one has been able to tell us so far what old Friedrich did in his earlier life. Was he a Nazi or not? We can only find out if we look. Stop giving me that look, I can already see the curiosity shining in your green eyes.« Nabih pondered for a few moments before putting on his characteristic grin and agreeing. At sunset, they returned fully loaded with their equipment and collapsed exhausted on a sand dune. There, they gazed dreamily up at the horizon, where an orange veil was visible, leaving them contemplative.

»Hey, Diyar, have you ever wondered if the play of colors in the sky is as beautiful in other parts of the world as it is with us?«

»Even if it is, nothing is as beautiful as the place where one grew up. I often think about how our lives would have turned out if it weren't for the war. The sad thing is that we'll soon leave the place where we learned to walk and talk. When you realize all of this, a feeling of helplessness overwhelms me, something that cannot be described with any words. How about you?«

»So many things are running through my mind. Some thoughts are so negative that I'm afraid of myself. I haven't talked to anyone in my family about it until now. Because we men have to be externally strong and must not show our feelings outwardly to protect the family. Our current situation can be compared to a pilot trying to save his plane from crashing while the engines are on fire. If he panics, he can't think clearly anymore, and his actions would be without any structure. And I think we need that structure so that we don't completely succumb to our fear. But as tragic as everything around us may be, hope always stands above all. That hope that will give us wings.« Diyar absorbed what was said and placed his hand on his friend's shoulder, who smiled encouragingly. Half an hour later, the sun had completely set. They carefully approached the spot where the stones were and lit their oil lamps, illuminating their immediate surroundings. Shovel by shovel, they dug into the soil, and suddenly Diyar was overcome by significant doubts.

»It's not right, what we're doing here.«

»Wait a moment. Did you think earlier that

we were going on vacation when we sweated through the sand here?«

»No, but...«

»How, but? What we're doing here is akin to desecrating a grave, and I, idiot that I am, let myself be swept away by you into this daring adventure. I'll give you two options. Either we put an end to this now, or we quietly disappear and just forget what happened. But don't take too long with your decision, my patience isn't particularly good today.« Diyar seemed to be having doubts and finally threw all his reservations overboard.

»Ah, whatever. Let's continue, my thirst for knowledge is greater than my cowardice, anyway.«

»That's what I wanted to hear. By the way, I was clear from the beginning that you wouldn't chicken out. You're just too curious for that.«

»You're solely to blame for that. If only I had continued to study dinosaurs, I wouldn't have become a shabby grave robber.«

»From your mouth, everything always sounds like those tales from One Thousand and One Nights. Next, the Sultan's daughter will probably come by on a flying carpet, singing you a love song.« A offended look was thrown over, and Nabih burst out laughing so loudly that he infected his friend with laughter. Shortly after, they hit solid ground, abruptly interrupting their merriment. Both immediately dropped to their knees and carefully continued digging with their hands until Diyar came across a bone, which he gently exposed. With an uneasy feeling, he nudged his friend, who looked up in astonishment.

»Okay, I take it all back. Maybe what you said is true. But one set of bones unfortunately doesn't prove anything.«

»You were born a skeptic. Look here, it continues.« Under a thin layer of clay, more bones emerged, gradually forming several skeletons. Next to them were some dog tags with stamped names and birthdates, as well as antique artifacts that strongly resembled their clay shard. Before they could exchange thoughts, a beam of light appeared, rapidly approaching. The two quickly climbed out of their hole and took cover behind the excavated sandbank as the vehicle came to a stop right in front of them. Whispering, they turned to each other, feverishly considering what to do, when a familiar voice rang out.

»Come out of your holes, you dirty thieves,

but quickly. Before I put an end to you. You have exactly ninety seconds.« Nabih turned chalk-white and whispered desperately to himself, while Diyar shook his head, watching.

»Oh shit, no, do you hear that accent? It must be old Friedrich. This Nazi pig will chop off our heads. Then he'll bury us, and our parents will never know what happened to us.«

»Shut up, you coward. No one is going to lose their heads here unless you cry even louder. But then, I'll personally deliver you. Yes, yes, it's always my fault. Where are your brilliant ideas when we're in trouble? Come on, share, I'm waiting.«

»On what? Do I look like a magician who can make us disappear with a snap of my fingers, you donkey? We're going to come out carefully and surrender. Just like the soldiers buried beneath us did.«

»Your suggestion sounds like a suicide mission. We might as well shoot ourselves.«

Nabih waited several seconds for a response. Then he impatiently turned to the side and reluctantly followed his friend, who emerged from cover with raised hands. Like deserters, they stood in the spotlight, trying to catch a glimpse into the darkness where they suspected the German was. After several minutes with no action, they became visibly uneasy and started whispering, prompting the lights to go out. Startled, Nabih screamed and, out of fear, made a mess in his pants, which the man approaching slowly took note of with satisfaction.

»Interesting, now I recognize you. Aren't you the boy who was in my shop this morning?

And you, little scaredy-cat with glasses, you once called me a Nazi. I've met many people in my life, but such treacherous bastards, I haven't encountered since the war. What possessed you to desecrate the grave of my comrades? Are you out of your minds? Whose idea was this?« Nabih immediately buckled and pointed directly at Diyar, who shot him an angry look.

»It's not what it seems.«

»Well, for me, it seems quite obvious. You wanted to plunder the resting place of my comrades. Is that right?«

»No, you completely misunderstand. I was at your shop today to ask if the clay shard I'm holding is genuine. But I was so scared that I left it there.«

»All right, that explains one thing. But why are you here with shovels and the sandbank in the background? That can't be a coincidence.«

»When I realized I had left it behind, we followed you. I just wanted to retrieve it, nothing more. The idea with the grave came later because we wanted to know if you really were a N...« He bit his tongue.

»An N...? You mean a Nazi?«

»Yes, exactly.«

»Heavens! This topic has been haunting me my entire life. And I will shed light on it once and for all. But first, you will close the pit again, understood?« Both immediately stood at attention and shoveled the sand back into the hole. Diyar whispered angrily towards his friend, who turned his face away in shame. Afterward, old Friedrich checked the pockets of the supposed grave robbers and went with them to his van, where they all sat down together on the loading platform.

»Who put the idea into your heads that I am a fascist, you miserable rascals? Your parents?« Diyar confirmed and continued to listen attentively.

»One should not always believe everything one's parents say. Before the war, they told me and my comrades that people who did not belong to our race were our enemies and had to be fought to the death. But when we went out with the company for our first mission, there was nothing there except the silence of the desert. No enemy, no race, just me and my blind, endless hatred that met no resistance. I was devastated and waited day in and day out for something to happen, but nothing did. Until after days, we finally came across a Bedouin, who was traversing the wilderness with his fully packed camels. I was the first to make contact with him, as I also worked in the army as a translator. He was extremely friendly and asked me why I was here? At the age of just twenty, I knew nothing about life. So, I deliberately avoided the question because, honestly, I had no answer. In between, he observed me curiously. His inquiring gaze inevitably fell on my army uniform embroidered with the swastika and my comrades in the background, with their rifles at the ready, shouting loudly to me.

»Come on, Leopold, get out of the way. We have the Indian in our sights.« The nomad immediately sensed that the mood could shift at any moment and told me something that would change my perspective forever. »The desert is like a heart that cannot exist without light.«

Subsequently, a shot rang out, hitting the local directly in the chest. Before I realized what had happened, he slumped lifelessly to the ground. Like hyenas, my comrades then pounced on the belongings of a peaceful man, whose blood slowly seeped into the dense sand. Although I was aware from the beginning of what war meant, I was not prepared for the pain and guilt that would accompany me from then on. From that moment on, my hatred transformed into something good because I wanted nothing to do with the coming crimes and my past. That same evening, we set up our camp. We all swayed in deceptive security, transformed by the abundant alcohol into a hazy veil of normality. Fortunately, due to my misbehavior in the morning, I had been sentenced to duty by my officer. Therefore, I did not drink and was the only one in our company who could still think rationally. Just before sunrise, my eyes closed. Exactly at that moment, we fell into an ambush, where all my comrades were liquidated. Paradoxically, they let me live. But during the subsequent torture I had to endure, they made it clear that we infidels had no place on their sacred land. For me, the war was over from that moment. I buried my comrades, changed my identity, and went into hiding for a long time. Eventually, I became one of them. No one knew who I was or where I came from, as I adopted their faith and mastered their language. It was only when you two curious birds appeared that speculations turned into facts, bringing that terrible time back to light.

»You, with the shard in hand, what is your name?«

»Me? I'm called Nabih.« he stammered.

»By the way, that means 'the wise.' So, I'll give you a well-meant advice that you should internalize. Bury the artifact as deep as you can and let it be.«

»But why? It's mine.«

»This gruesome thing is responsible for endless bloodshed and comes from looting that occurred due to the war. The artifacts in the grave once belonged to the Bedouin killed by my comrades. There's even a rumor that those relics carry the souls of their ancestors and are therefore cursed. You can, of course, keep it, but it's practically worthless, as no one will buy it from you.« The facial expressions of the two spoke volumes, which is why the old man inquired more precisely.

»I've been wondering all this time, why are

you holding onto it so tightly? Is there any reason?« Diyar immediately took the lead and looked over to Nabih, who seemed visibly disappointed, staring into the void.

»We found it many years ago near the old military base and wanted to sell it to finance the escape of my best friend.«

»Men, I can understand your actions to some extent, but there are far more honorable ways to make money.«

»That may be true. But time is running out for us. The war is advancing rapidly, and I cannot allow my better half to be left behind. My heart could never bear that.« Monsieur Friedrich left the statement unanswered and pointed out into the distance. There, on the horizon, a white eagle could be seen, gliding without a single flap of its wings in the dazzling light of the sunrise.

A Legend Named Jaroud

As the old curmudgeon curiously asked how the story continued, suddenly the outboard motor roared to life in the background. In response, the majority of people sent up one prayer of thanks after another into the night sky. Some of them, however, simply sat there, clutching their children or indulging in memories that gave them strength and hope.

»Besides the fact that I need to apologize to you, Diyar, I'm glad that the rickety box finally started up and we won't end up as fish food.« Zainab, holding her little Adil tightly and conveying to the gloomy painter with a disdainful expression that she did not approve of his statement.

»Please don't look at me so angrily with

your big green eyes. I'm nicer than I look, even if I occasionally go too far with my gallows humor.«

»Yes, at least you noticed that I didn't find it funny.«

»Alright, I apologize to you. But please, tell your little one not to look so malicious, it's quite frightening. By the way, my name is Bassem. I only tell you that so you don't call me old scruff until the end of our journey. I really don't deserve that.«

»Interesting? The name means something like laughter. That explains why you try to be funny.«

All three looked at each other amused, momentarily forgetting their worries, before Bassem glanced over at Diyar with interest.

»Even though it might not be the appropriate moment, I still wanted to know what happened to Nabih and why he can't be with us?« Diyar stared thoughtfully out at the open sea, visibly struggling to find the right words.

»It's extremely difficult for me to talk about it right now. How about you tell us a bit about yourself first? That might take my mind off things." Bassem was about to start his story when Zainab pointed to her son and the other boy, who were sitting on the floor of the boat communicating with gestures.

»That's beautiful to watch. You see, the language of children is universal, no matter where they come from. Now, let me tell you a bit about myself so we can get to know each other better. I am a simple man, hailing from the once-green north, who never really asked much from life. The reason being that nothing around me existed to change my perspective. It's important not to forget that I grew up in a time when people still worked hard in the fields and had to plant and harvest what they ate with their own hands. There were no schools, no formal education as we know it today. All the knowledge was passed down to us by our fathers, who took us out to work at a young age. Tradition held immense value. No one would ever dare to defy or contradict the head of the family. When the eldest spoke, everyone without exception followed, regardless of whether they agreed or not. Over the years, progress gradually advanced. Many of my former friends left our village and sought their fortunes in the surrounding cities that sprouted up like mushrooms thanks to industrialization. However, some of them returned because they missed the freedom and peace that the hustle and bustle of the big city had taken from them. No matter what adventures people told me about over the years, I was always content with what God had given me and never felt the longing to leave this place. All that mattered to me was providing a sheltered life for my children, whom I wanted to give a better livelihood.

During times of prosperity, we received high-profile visits from the president, who promised us the world along with his entourage. He gave us land, the fields of which could not be culti-vated as they had completely dried up due to years of drought. With a confident voice, he spoke of the flourishing future of our country and indirectly demanded that we submit to his grand power fantasies. Like many before me, I also trusted his words, which led me to not question anything and become a blind follower. Thanks to good relations, trade flourished with the world powers, from whom we bought weapons paid for with oil that actually belonged to the starving people. To distract from his internal problems, he instigated wars against neighboring states. Gradually, brave citizens turned against the tyrannical despot, whose resistance he fiercely crushed with the help of the military. Many of the insurgents were murdered or imprisoned, where they were used to dig mass graves that grew day by day due to the senseless dying on the battlefields. All of this happened under the watchful eye of the West, which delivered mass supplies of its deadly cargo. At the annual state banquet, amidst caviar and wine, they sealed their solidarity with a firm handshake made of the blood of the victims. Many years earlier, in times of peace, due to the lack of prospects, I decided to send our children to the army. My wife and I had a bad feeling from the start, which would prove to be correct many years later. Because shortly after the war began, my sons were ordered to the front. I knew I had to act quickly, so I drove to the military base that same night, where I demanded entry in vain. I parked my car nearby and called out the names of my sons, Ahmed and Nader, to every troop transporter leaving the compound for the front. Fortunately, my desperate call finally found a response at sunrise. When my boys saw me, they jumped off the loading platform and threw their weapons into the sand. We quickly moved away from the scene and stopped outside the city, where we managed to shake off the military police. For minutes, we embraced each other and searched for a solution, knowing that time was running out. Nader was extremely well-read and had a good general knowledge, which is why he was called a professor within the family. Ahmed was a calm character with an analytical mind, which complemented each other perfectly.

Completely bewildered, I stood that morning between my men who were excitedly discussing with each other. After countless suggestions, we finally came to a solution that led us to an old acquaintance who lived far away, high up in the mountains. Upon our arrival, we cautiously stepped out of the car, immediately drawing the attention of the residents who recognized our origin by our license plate. At that time, the regime ruled its country with an iron fist. This imaginary threat loomed like a sword of Damocles over the heads of the population, who increasingly distrusted each other. Suddenly, everyone seemed suspicious, resulting in citizens spying on each other out of fear of falling out of favor. With trembling knees, I knocked on the door of my former friend, who looked at me in surprise. While I explained my situation to him, my boys hid, as I had to ensure that I could trust my counterpart. After listening to me, he finally took us into his house. However, he made it clear to me that we could only stay for a few days, as the risk of being arrested was too high. While my sons slept, I kept watch and observed like an eagle the vehicles driving up the switchbacks from the valley. After three days without sleep, I was so tired that

I suddenly saw things and heard things that simply didn't make sense. Rocks turned into people, and a gust of wind brushing the trees turned into voices incessantly talking to me. My thinking was increasingly dominated by my fear, which is why I eventually decided to move on. At our farewell, my old friend uttered the following sentence, which still gives me goosebumps today.

»My prayers are with you. I hope you encounter Jaroud. Without, you won't make it to the border.« Before we continued over the mountains, I called my wife one last time. I handed the phone to Nader and Ahmed, after which all barriers broke down, and they began to cry desperately. At the end of the conversation, I managed to somewhat calm her down, but only because I promised to come home safely. Completely exhausted, we fought our way through rugged terrain. After a long and arduous march through remote mountain paths, we finally rested. While consuming our rations, we looked down at a small town, high up, surrounded by several combat helicopters. Due to my sons concerns, we decided to stay where we were and continue the next day. We spent the night under the open sky, sleeping under a densely overgrown tree that gave us a sense of security.

Early in the morning, we were awakened by the roar of fighter jets plunging through the cloud cover. In one motion, we jumped up and looked down at the city in horror as they dropped their deadly cargo. After the explosion, dark plumes of smoke rose, initially white, then black, and finally yellow. Anxiously, I looked over at my sons, who alerted me to the putrid smell gradually creeping into our noses. Shortly after, the lively activity came to a sudden halt. First, the birdsong ceased, then a large number of people fell lifeless to the ground. Shocked, I gazed into the valley, overcome by the eerie silence, completely paralyzing me.

Some managed to escape somehow. They ran with their children in tow for their lives toward the north, only to be overtaken by the deadly cloud of gas carried by the wind. For minutes, we stood motionless on the edge of the abyss when, out of nowhere, a shepherd extended his hand with the following words.

»Jaroud.« I was completely beside myself and followed the stranger with my sons, who took us to his hut. At first, none of us felt like speaking. But then it burst out of me, accusing our immediate neighbors of the cowardly attack. He refuted my claim and reminded me that no one but our country had access to these new types of aircraft. The sheer horror rose within me, haunting me throughout the day. Late at night, I sneaked away because I wanted to see the terrible course the events had taken. From a distance, you could clearly see the bodies, thousands lined up under the lights of the street lamps. Although the distance was relatively large, you could still hear the desperate cries of the relatives, echoing in my thoughts to this day. On the way back, a shiver overcame me, one that simply wouldn't let go. I tried to somehow explain the whole thing to myself and eventually failed due to the sheer cruelty that made my mind recoil. Upon arriving at the house, I lay down. Everything was spinning until I finally fell asleep after a chaotic whirl-wind of thoughts. In my dream, I relived the attack. I stood amidst the chaos that suddenly spread after the detonations. A man ran towards me with his children in his arms, shouting, "Gas! Gas!" before they collapsed lifelessly. Others hurriedly made their way to their cars, closed the windows, and raced away in a hurry. On their way out of the city, they drove over dozens of dead bodies strewn across the streets in their own vomit. Shortly after, I smelled the scent of sweet apples, and I woke up drenched in sweat. At daybreak, the army arrived. In the distance, I heard muffled shots as Ahmed and Nader came running, completely distraught, reporting on scouts. They were in their SUVs, using their binoculars to systematically search the mountain regions for refugees. It dawned on me immediately that we needed to act quickly, so we left our hiding place shortly thereafter. Although the shepherd seemed aware of the dangers, he still took us to a renegade path that separated the border regions by a raging river.

Freedom seemed within reach, and before I could make a decision, the soldiers caught up with us in their vehicles. At first, they mistook us for ordinary refugees. However, when they saw my sons' army boots, they knew they were deserters. With our hands raised, we stood at the edge of the ravine and let our lives pass before our eyes with a petrified gaze into the barrels of the machine guns. To my surprise, nothing happened for a while. But then someone pulled the trigger and shot down the shepherd, whose body hit the rocky ground with a loud thud. Seizing the brief moment of distraction, I pushed my sons with all my strength into the river several meters below us. Fortunately, the rapids swiftly carried them away, causing the bullets to miss their mark. Praying loudly to God, I closed my eyes and waited for my execution. It wasn't until I heard them securing their rifles and the SUV slowly moving away that I realized they had spared me for some reason. For several days, I desperately searched the border area. But all I found was Nader's formerly white shirt soaked in blood.

As I arrived home early in the morning, I was faced with the ruins of my existence. Everything had been bombed to the ground except for the foundations. One of my neighbors approached me directly upon my arrival. I can still vividly remember his broken expression, which immediately plunged me into a state of shock. Through tears, he recounted that several rockets had struck our neighborhood during the night, one of which hit our house. Everyone immediately rushed to the scene and cleared away the rubble until they came across the lifeless body of my wife, who was futilely resuscitated on the spot. I didn't react and felt the spoken words piercing directly into my heart. My sons had disappeared without a trace, and the love of my life had forever departed from me. Bassem visibly struggled with his emotions and was on the verge of interrupting his narrative when Zainab reached for his hand.

All of this was more than thirty years ago now, yet it feels like it was just yesterday. People seemingly don't learn from their mistakes, hence the repetition of history, with fleeing and displacement occurring over and over again. Eventually, I found myself confronted with the harsh reality when my brother told me that I should stop believing in miracles because my sons would never return.

When the war resumed a few months ago, he took all his savings and fled abroad with his family. I wrapped up everything and also decided to leave my homeland. I traveled from the north to the south in just under a week. On my final stretch, I encountered a boy guarding a roadblock in army uniform. He wore glasses, had curly hair, and was extremely talkative.

Suddenly, Diyar became attentive and looked curiously, suspecting it might be Nabih. After a friendly greeting, he advised me not to proceed further as rebels were entrenched in the buildings ahead, shooting at anything that moved.

After a brief consideration, he took me under his wing and eventually guided me through the dangerous zone where one could constantly hear gunfire from the nearby combat. Although I had long left my life behind, I constantly feared that I wouldn't make it. I prayed inwardly and startled at my own cowardice. Meanwhile, the boy beside me bravely surveyed the immediate surroundings and cared for the well-being of a total stranger. During the night we spent together in hiding, I asked him his name and what wishes he had for the future. However, he evaded the question repeatedly and talked about trivial matters, while his words settling like an insurmountable barrier on his soul. At daybreak, he safely escorted me to the harbor, which was controlled by the army, appearing overwhelmed and disorganized. Hundreds of refugees stood around, unsure of what would happen next. As we bid farewell, I saw some of the tension leave him. He confided in me that he was determined to get on one of those boats at any cost. But just as he was about to tell me his name, a crowd of people surged between us, and I lost sight of him.

Diyar was torn by the story and burst with curiosity.

»That must have been my friend Nabih. No one has as pure a heart as he does. How long ago was this, and why didn't you look for him?«

»About three weeks ago. Trust me, I did. But the chaos was just too much.« Shortly after, Zainab interjected with a question that had been bothering her all along.

»Who is this 'Jaroud' you mentioned several times?«

»Jaroud isn't a person. Jaroud is a word that comes from a legend found only in the northern dialect of the mountain dwellers, meaning 'The Good within You.' Anyone who helps others in times of need can be a 'Jaroud'. You or even I.«

»Or Nabih and your sons«. Diyar added proudly, earning a gentle nod from Bassem.

The President's Bomb

During the night, strong winds arose, and the sea became rougher by the minute. Everyone held on as best they could, suddenly exposed to the primal force of nature that rocked the boat wildly like a nutshell. Some became chalk-white and battled their nausea until they had to vomit. Despite the uncertainty on their faces, the guy steering the outboard motor remained unfazed and skillfully maneuvered the boat between the foam crests of the waves. After the sea had calmed somewhat, little Adil wriggled out of his mother's arms and walked over to the daring helmsman, eyeing him curiously. Just as Zainab was about to get up, Bassem winked at Diyar, who had positioned himself behind the runaway for safety.

»Don't worry, your son won't fall over-board, he has his protector with him. Look, your boy seems to have infected the other kids. Now the helsman at least has something to do until the end of our journey and can answer unnecessary questions.«

»Well, that's a relief, but I'll still keep an eye on him, you never know.«

»Yeah, go ahead.«

»Excuse me, but there's something weigh-ing on my mind that I wanted to discuss with you alone. However, I'm not sure if it's too per-sonal.«

»Even if you don't like to hear it, my dear, nobody knows what tomorrow holds. So, go ahead and ask your question. We have all the time in the world.« Zainab hesitated for a few seconds but then gathered herself.

»How did you cope with the loss of your wife? I ask because I lost my husband, and not a second goes by without my heart being full of sorrow.«

»You know, we humans always want to deal with things we can't control. But have you ever wondered why we even want to deal with the pain or loss that causes us so much grief?«

»To be honest, no.«

»Well, as long as we confront and deal with something we can't master, we're in constant conflict, fighting against it internally. This costs an extreme amount of energy, something some people eventually break under. I've been at this point in my life several times too.«

»Yes, and how did you overcome the pain?«

»I didn't overcome it. I accepted it as a part

of me. Please internalize the following. Emotions are like words. They're only as powerful as the attention you give them. And without attention, they're practically nonexistent.«

»The more I think about it, the more I understand what you're saying. But what scares me is this. I always fear that if I don't confront the loss, I might lose the connection to my husband.« With a smile, Bassem pointed to little Adil, who happily ran around, radiating pure joy.

»Your child is the reason why you'll never forget your husband. He's the link that holds you three together forever.«

»Thank you, that means a lot to me.«

»You've piqued my curiosity. Would you mind telling me your beloved's name and what happened to him? I'm deeply touched by other people's stories, and I feel connected to them through it.«

»My husband's name was Salim.« she said proudly.

»That name is simply beautiful, just like its meaning. Please, continue.«

»I hadn't seen him for more than three months by that time, as he was working underground. My husband was an aspiring journalist, employed by a small newspaper. He always had a premonition that the regime-critical articles he had been writing for years would eventually be censored or even banned. His suspicion became a reality shortly after, on a sunny day in May, when several people barged into his office and attacked him without warning. Salim knew that the message was just a taste of what was to come. Without any fear, he continued his work, until one day the secret police showed up at our door. From there, everything fell apart. After a fleeing across the country, he went into hiding, from where he continued his work.

I was arrested by the police, thrown into prison, where they tried to extract a confession from me and tortured me in every imaginable way. Endless nights of hope and fear passed until they finally released me. Despite my injuries from the abuse, my first thought was of my son. Without hesitation, I went straight to my parents, who lovingly cared for Adil during my imprisonment. With a heavy heart, I returned to our house the next morning and burned every single document that could incriminate us behind closed curtains. Late at night, I heard a faint knock. Armed with a knife, I stood at the apartment door, under which someone un-known pushed a letter. After making sure the coast was clear, I opened the letter, in which my husband spoke of fears and hopes. I cried with-out interruption and stared hypnotized at the piece of paper, on which my tears fell in sec-onds." "A few minutes later, I had somewhat composed myself again. That's when I noticed the address written in tiny letters at the bottom left corner. Without hesitation, I grabbed Adil and set off for the small town over a hundred kilometers away. Upon our arrival, I pulled my headscarf down deep into my face and avoided any eye contact, as I suspected government thugs behind every corner. Just before we ap-proached the destination, I was approached by a stranger, whom I passed silently. Then I heard footsteps, getting faster and faster. At first, my panic was still manageable. But then, my heart rate skyrocketed, and I ran back towards the marketplace as if possessed, blending into the bustling crowd. I kept looking back paranoidly until I gathered the courage again and visited the given address. Just before I knocked on the door, someone tapped me on the shoulder from behind with the following words.«

»Zaini, why did you run away? Don't you recognize your husband anymore?« I immediately threw myself into Salim's arms, whispering and crying into his ear.

»Well, no wonder if you're talking to strange women in dark alleys.« He laughed and walked with us into the house. However, the joy of reunion lasted only briefly. After he had put our child to bed, he confessed something to me that once again shook my world.

»Please, be strong now, I need to tell you something important. There are documents in my office that I urgently need.«

»What do you mean?«

»Before they wanted to arrest me, a former officer came to my office. At first, I was skeptical and didn't quite know what he wanted from me, as he kept his statements extremely vague. However, the conversation took an interesting turn when he slid over strictly confidential documents he carried around in an inconspicuous plastic bag. I suspiciously examined the content, which made my heart race from page to page, as it was explosive material signed by the president himself. My counterpart was well-versed and knew that I had very good contacts, which is why he proposed a deal. This involved smuggling his entire family out of the country, in exchange for which he let me read the files.«

»Tell me you didn't agree to this dubious offer?« Zainab asked incredulously.

»I'm a journalist, I had no choice. The truth is my top priority, especially since it could likely save the lives of thousands of people.«

»But you're also a husband and father, or did you forget that?«

»Of course not. I'm doing all this for us. The dire situation we're in has nothing to do with the exchange deal. I have to fear for my life anyway, and it would be nice if you could support me in this one thing.« When I heard that, my legs became so weak that I collapsed to the ground powerless. It took some time before I could muster the strength to get up and think clearly again. All I ever longed for was a stable family life, which now seemed to be slipping further away.

»I'll never leave you, but you must tell me what the content is and what I need to do.«

»The documents are contracts concluded years ago with a European country for the construction of a nuclear facility. The research reactor ILIB and the megawatt breeder are already completed and are set to go online as nuclear facilities, in a few weeks."

»What's so bad about that? Then we'll finally have no more electricity problems.«

»Please don't be so naive. The reactor is merely a distraction. Because with the over twelve kilograms of uranium delivered, our country intends to build an atomic bomb. This would make our president the most powerful autocrat in the Middle East and could, with the snap of his fingers, take any of our neighboring countries hostage. This would influence the balance of power for decades, and his sick power fantasies would progress even faster. That's why you have to go to my office early tomorrow morning and grab the documents. So that a middleman can smuggle them quickly out of the country. Do you understand that so far?«

»Yes, but I wonder why you're not sending someone else for this delicate task. Someone who maybe doesn't have a family and wouldn't be hit so hard by the punishment in case of arrest.«

»You know why. Firstly, because you're the only person on this planet whom I trust. And secondly, because none of my former colleagues would betray you. You just stroll in, have my office unlocked, and casually walk out with the documents. It won't take five minutes. While I'm currently looking after Adil.«

»My dearest, that all sounds so simple. But what if something goes wrong and the documents aren't where they originally were? Wait, where the hell are they anyway?«

»Wait, that panicked look on your face just reminded me of the day before our wedding. When you cried all day because you thought you wouldn't fit into the dress.«

»It feels exactly like that. Except now the dress has turned into a bomb that could explode at any moment.«

»I would laugh if the situation weren't so serious. Behind the picture of the president is a small safe that opens with our child's birthdate. Inside, you'll find everything you need.«

Zainab took a deep breath, while Bassem attentively hung on her lips, following the story with anticipation.

Early in the morning, I stood in front of the inconspicuous house where my husband's office was located. With sweaty hands, I opened the entrance door and walked past the reception, where mustachioed Ali still sat, greeting me with surprise. I headed straight for the elevator. But when I saw the many people, panic seized me, so I ran up the stairs to the third floor. Salim's office was within reach, at the other end of the corridor. Carefully, I took one step after another when out of nowhere an old colleague of my husband's turned the corner. Her exuberant greeting attracted the attention of the entire department. Completely unsettled, I suddenly found myself in the hustle and bustle, where I completely lost track, not knowing who was new and whom I could trust. But apparently, I was so good at lying that they left me alone after a short time and unlocked the office for me without being asked. Inside, I headed straight for the gold-framed picture of the president. In no time, I had gained access to the safe and pulled out everything I could find. The top-secret documents, a pistol, and a thick bundle of dollar bills, of which I wondered where they came from or to whom they belonged. I hid everything under my dress and left the office purposefully, where mustachioed Ali seized me with a firm grip. During my imprisonment, a lot of anger had built up. Anger that unleashed unexpected strength and turned into a targeted kick that landed in the soft parts of my opponent. I was amazed at myself and at the same time filled with guilt. At first, I wanted to help the whimpering weakling back on his feet, but then he screamed for help at the top of his lungs, causing me to run like crazy. As I ran, I kept turning around and saw someone else trailing behind me. Instinctively, I reached for the gun and shot recklessly behind me. Suddenly, screams were heard everywhere. It became chaotic. People ran around in panic and streamed towards the exit, among whom I found myself. Outside the door, I immediately got into a taxi and left the scene. Spellbound, I took one last look over my shoulder and felt immense relief as the house in the background became smaller and smaller. On the way, I changed vehicles several times until I arrived back at the house just after midnight. I was still full of adrenaline and furious at my husband, whom I greeted with a resounding slap. Shocked, he held his cheek and waited for my reaction.

»What did you expect? A lie always provokes a reaction, and if I didn't love you so much, I would have strangled you.« she gestured furiously.

»Probably I don't deserve anything else. But believe me, I had to sugarcoat the whole thing for you, even though I didn't feel particularly good about it. The truth would have only made you nervous.«

»Not feel particularly good about it? I was sweating blood and water, and when leaving your office, mustachioed Ali held me back, to whom I left a nice farewell gift. Honestly, I couldn't stand that horny bastard anyway.

Then I had to shoot around and flee in the chaos.«

»What? That's not like you at all. I hope you didn't hurt anyone?«

»Shows you what torture and your lies can do to someone. Let's not talk too much about details now, your colleagues are all safe. Instead, check if everything is complete. I'll go check on the little one in the meantime.« Salim flipped through the documents page by page and carefully photographed everything as Zainab returned.

»What are you doing? I thought we were done with the covert mission.«

»That would be nice. I need to make sure the documents get safely out of the country so we can prevent the disaster in time. I'll give you the film. I'll hand over the documents to a middleman in the morning, who is already on his way to us.«

»To be honest, I have serious doubts about this.«

»I believe you, I told you the truth after all.«

»Yes, but this time it feels different some-how.«

»Don't stress yourself out, you've already risked your life enough today. Tomorrow it's my turn. «

»You say that so jokingly. I can't laugh about it at all.«

»If it comforts you, you can take a walk with our son in the meantime. And now off to bed, I'm about to collapse from exhaustion.«
The whole night, I couldn't close my eyes. I kept getting up and peering out from behind the curtains, as the eerie silence weighed heavily on

me. Just before sunrise, I woke up my son and kissed Salim goodbye as he left. While making my rounds, a dark car with tinted windows passed me near the marketplace. At first, I didn't think much of it, but then I hurried back and watched from a distance as the vehicle came to a stop in front of our house. Salim politely invited the gentlemen in, who looked somehow menacing with their sunglasses and black suits. Several minutes passed before anything happened. What unfolded was exactly what I had warned my husband about the night before. In handcuffs, he was escorted away by the shady figures, causing me to nearly have a nervous breakdown.

Once the car had disappeared, I returned to the house. There, I grabbed the film and the bundle of money.

Suddenly, an incredible determination surged through me to complete my husband's mission. With tears in my eyes, I headed towards the nearest telephone booth and, after a short search, dialed the number of a Western embassy. However, the phone call went quite differently than I had expected, so I got into a taxi and personally drove to the address provided. When I received no response to my frantic ringing, I wrote a brief letter. I placed it along with the film in an envelope, on the outside of which, in my anger and desperation, I wrote "The President's Bomb". Due to the situation, I avoided going home, fearing I might be arrested again. However, after weeks of being on the run, the longing became too much, so I returned. There, I found one last letter from Salim, which made

it clear that I had to leave our homeland immediately.

*"Dear Zaini, if you're reading this letter, they've al-
ready arrested me. Please don't despair when I tell
you that I won't return to you alive. The money in
the safe, I've saved it for your escape. Most likely,
they'll hunt you down. So, do me the favor and leave
our home as soon as you read this letter, heading towards the port. There, you'll find enough smugglers
who will get you out of the country for a few hundred dollars. Regardless of the situation you're facing, I have to say goodbye to both of you now. You
know, I've never been someone who liked to put my
thoughts and feelings on paper. But now, I have no
choice. Everything I know about love, you've taught
me. I'm infinitely grateful and at the same time filled
with sadness that I'll never be able to hold Adil and
you in my arms again. Our last kiss was the end and*

also the beginning of a beautiful journey that I will never forget."

Despite the unspeakable melancholy, Zainab remained outwardly composed and continued speaking without interruption. When I arrived at the harbor in the evening, I settled down in a small café with Adil, where I watched the television news. There, it was reported about an attack by several foreign fighter jets on an industrial area in the East. They flew so closely together that they were mistaken for a passenger plane on the radar, and therefore no countermeasures were taken. Although my mind was elsewhere, the news immediately brought me back to reality. Attentively, I listened to the conversation of the older gentlemen next to me, who jokingly spoke of a secret facility for building an atomic bomb. From that point on, it gradually became clear to me that my action with the embassy had likely borne fruit. Meanwhile, the other refugees had also moved closer and were eagerly watching Zainab, who brought her story to life with vivid imagery.

Every Fate Counts

Several hours passed before someone dared to voice their concerns.

»I've been listening to some of you for a while now, but this somber silence between the sentences is simply unbearable. Do you really believe we'll make it across this rickety boat unharmed? Just recently, I heard from an old acquaintance that someone on a converted fishing boat, with over three hundred souls aboard, was swallowed by the depths. His tale deeply affected me since my own journey was imminent.« Everyone looked down, unwilling to confront the idea of death.

»Even if you turn away from me, it doesn't change the fact that in a few hours, we might not be here anymore. What's sad is that nowadays, we aren't even worth a headline. It's like in war. Initially, names are mentioned, then only numbers are spoken of.«

»Yeah, and why do you think that is?« shouted someone excitedly.

»Think about it! Every day, thousands flee their homelands, and many of them lose their lives. In the eyes of the West, we're nothing but byproducts causing more cost than benefit. We're not billionaires diving in a submarine to the ocean's depths or joyfully planting flags atop the world's highest peak. People are desensitized, seeking light entertainment that doesn't provoke thought. Yet, we must fight for survival every day, confronted with our fate. You've heard about Diyar's experiences, haven't you?«

»But that doesn't mean we have to listen to

a rebellious woman. Sometimes, one has to turn away from reality to avoid being sucked into the vortex deep within our souls. And now, I suggest you shut your mouth before your pessimism capsizes our boat.« Bassem observed the situation closely, refraining from intervening as he wanted to see how the young lady would stand her ground against an adult. She didn't yield and continued to hold her own until the man lost his temper and forcefully shoved her off the boat. Everyone startled at once, looking frightened, while the helmsman swiftly turned the wheel and pulled the young woman, who was on the verge of drowning, out of the waters. Drenched, the rescuer stepped forward before the refugees and vented his anger.

»Are you all out of your minds? You're

lucky it's a full moon and the sea's relatively calm. I couldn't care less about who's to blame, but instead of fighting each other, you should stick together. And this is the last time I turn back for one person, risking everyone's lives. Got it? If so, get that shivering one some dry clothes pronto. Then she'll tell us the story of the sunken trawler, a tale I'd very much like to hear.« Just as someone was about to offer their sweater, the attacker stepped forward in shame, handing his jacket and pants to the young woman, who started speaking after changing. Initially, her demeanor and voice were reserved, but as she delved deeper into her story, that changed. For over twenty years, Ibrahim sailed out to the open sea. He was a quiet man who was comfortable being alone and preferred the company of nature over that of humans. Initially, he seemed intimidated by the silence and endless expanse before him. However, over time, he became accustomed to the environment that provided him with peace and freedom. Every day, before sunrise, he cast his nets, hauling them in a few hours later. As he slowly navigated upstream with his fresh catch, the first traders gathered at the dock, mingling and exchanging the latest news over their morning coffee. When Ibrahim's fishing boat appeared on the horizon, he sounded the signal horn twice, prompting everyone to line up in the order they arrived. Upon docking, a sun-tanned, fully-bearded seventy-year-old sailor named Omar was always ready to secure the line around the bollard and receive the goods.

»There you are, finally, my friend, quite

late today.« he pointed at his watch.

»Stop the chatter and lend a hand.« Ibrahim replied.

»Your mood was never the best, but today it's particularly bleak.«

»If you knew what's going on out there. Since foreign ships are depleting our stocks, I have to venture farther out just to get something. A few days ago, they headed straight for me, wanting to sink my boat, claiming I was in their territory. If our government doesn't intervene and stop these criminals soon, I'll have to find another source of income.«

»Is the situation really that serious?«

»Hey, if I hadn't reacted quickly, my boat would've been firewood.«

»Okay, calm down, got it.«

»You're lucky to have lived in golden times.

You didn't have a problem with overfishing. Squids and lobsters willingly went into your nets.«

»Let's just say we had no complaints.«

»Oh, how I wish I could have lived in those times.«

»Sorry, but that's history now. Have you thought about what you'll do if you're no longer doing your regular work?«

»Well, I'll do what the shipping companies did during the war. They found a new target audience and converted their luxury liners into mobile transporters. And since we have plenty of compatriots who need to flee, I'll make a fortune on the side.«

»Not that you'll rename your cutter to Titanic.« Omar joked.

»Firstly, I'm missing four smokestacks for

that, and secondly, the name wouldn't be particularly trustworthy.«

»Do you have no guilt about your plan?«

»No, why should I? I could hope for better days and watch as life for my family and me goes to the dogs. If you're interested, feel free to lend a hand. I could use all the help I can get. Besides, nobody knows these waters as well as you do.«

»Well, I'm not that knowledgeable. After all, I've sailed the same route for forty years. Let me discuss this with my wife first, then I can tell you more.«

»With your wife? A man as big and strong as a bear doesn't need permission from his wife. And I always thought you were the epitome of masculinity. I must have been mistaken.« It was clear that Omar was trying hard to maintain his composure, eventually setting aside his doubts.

»I'm in, but only if the money's right.«

»Since the risk falls on both of us, I suggest we split it fifty-fifty.«

»If your mood matched your generosity, I'd probably end up empty-handed. But with that offer, I can't refuse.«

»But today, you'll have to help me unload. I'll let you know soon how things will proceed.«

Two weeks later, the first people from the remotest corners of the country arrived at the port with their belongings. They sought contact with the smugglers, encountering Ibrahim and his companion Omar. They were among the first to use a converted fishing boat for transporting refugees. Most crossings went smoothly, save for a few minor incidents. The business thrived. Until the competition among them became so intense that prices plummeted overnight. Ibrahim realized he needed to act fast. That's why he chose to load his boat to the brink, no longer taking thirty to forty refugees per trip, but cramming it full until it was bursting at the seams.

This decision led to constant friction between them as Omar's conscience increasingly made itself known.

»We need to stop this immediately. Your greed has clouded your judgment. You're cramming women and children below deck and into the engine room without any regard for their safety. Our bow is barely above water. What if the next big wave hits us? Will you take responsibility for the disaster then?«

»Interesting, first, you followed the call of money, and now suddenly, your conscience surfaces. We've had numerous crossings already, and not once have we been in real danger. Just look outside, the sea today is like a village pond. I couldn't care less about the people. This is about business, and I have to look out for myself.«

»Couldn't care less? How can someone be so heartless and greedy? In my eyes, these are all fates we're transporting, and each one matters to me.«

»Come on, spare me. You know what your problem is? You can never have enough. With godless creatures like you, one has to be damn careful because they drag everyone else down with them. I won't stand by you on this journey, you can do it alone.«

»Yeah, get lost, old man. I'm better off without your constant nagging.« As Ibrahim left the harbor, he searched for a helper he quickly identified amid the hustle and bustle of the crowd. Uncomfortably, Omar watched the green-painted fishing boat chug heavily into the evening glow. As he arrived home, the weather deteriorated rapidly. He was plagued by terrible guilt, which led him to turn back halfway and borrow a fellow fisherman's boat to trace his former partner's route. To minimize the risk, they hugged the coastline before veering out to the open sea. At the far end stood the ruins of an ancient temple, its six pillars towering ten meters high into the sky. A man named Quin once lived there, revered by his people as a visionary whose profound thoughts delved into the evolution of the human mind, shaped by both personal and foreign philosophies. Every four years, the greatest thinkers from neighboring lands gathered there, exchanging their teachings for weeks. After his passing, ongoing wars caused the once-significant place to fade into obscurity until more than a hundred years ago, when a handful of pilgrims rediscovered it. In the center of the temple, a marble panel was erected in honor of Quin, bearing an inscription that read:

"To be in the moment means to have a mind unbound by experiences of the past. Such a person is free from the process of thought, thus inexhaustible in energy."

Omar swiftly left the mainland behind, venturing further into the darkness. He stood at the helm, intensely focused, battling through towering waves that obscured his view with spray. After several hours when the weather calmed, he could see an oil slick and objects floating on the water's surface in the moonlight. With a foreboding feeling, he approached the scene, immediately spotting Ibrahim, who seemed to be the sole survivor, desperately calling for help. Omar was struck by a kind of shock, staring blankly into space. Although he had mentally prepared himself countless times for this moment, he couldn't contain the rush of emotions, tears streaming down his cheeks. Instead of pulling his former partner from the waters, he reached for the stuffed toy floating nearby.

»Don't even think about reaching for the boat. You've crossed the devil, now you have to face the consequences.«

»Come on, pull me up, I've realized my mistake.«

»Do you see the bear in my hand? You should be whimpering with guilt.

But all you do is think of yourself.«

»Please, I don't want to die.« he pleaded.

»Unlike the refugees, you had a choice. The choice of decision-making. These people were desperate and blindly trusted you. But to you, that seemed completely irrelevant because all you saw were dollar signs.«

»What are you talking about? You can't just leave me here.«

»Here, at the deepest point of the sea, it's five thousand meters down. It's just as dark down there as it is in your soul.«

»You wretched hypocrite. You're not in a position to tell me about my soul.«

»Maybe not me, but your Creator certainly is.« Ibrahim knew his last hour had come and paddled frantically towards the boat, reaching in vain for the ladder that hung out of his reach.

Exhausted, he slipped back into the water and looked up at his former partner, who started the engine and drove away. Two days later, news of the tragedy spread. Relatives wandered around the harbor, crying bitterly, praying, and hoping for good news. Amidst the despair, Omar sat dejected on a bollard, looking out to the open sea, thinking of the many victims he could have saved from death. Among all the tragedy surrounding him, there was a man who tearfully embraced his younger brother, the sole survivor of the disaster. However, the weight of helplessness became so heavy that night that Omar retreated to his home and took his own life with a revolver. The assailant who had previously pushed the young woman into the waters was so distraught by the story that he repeatedly apologized for his actions. This earned him the respect of all, although behind closed doors, some referred to him as 'The Confused Trouser-less Man.'

One Last Adventure

Shortly after, Bassem tapped Diyar on the shoulder. Who was in conversation with the young woman, who introduced herself as Amira after sharing her touching story.

»Sorry to interrupt. What about you? Will you tell us what happened next with Nabih?« Diyar hesitated visibly and eventually gave in to the many curious faces eagerly awaiting his words. As the sun set, Monsieur Friedrich sent us home. He stayed behind for a while, wanting to savor the moment of silence all to himself. Nabih's mood on the way home was more than somber. He kept looking over with a troubled expression through his round glasses, waiting for a reaction.

»As hard as it may sound, at the moment, I don't have a solution to our problem. But let me tell you one thing, I will never let you down.« Diyar encouraged his friend.

»That's good to hear because with all the hopelessness inside me, it's really not easy to stay positive. Do you think maybe old Friedrich might lend us a hand?« Nabih inquired.

»Hmm, that would be nice, but in life, unfortunately, we don't always get what we wish for. The dust on his antiques is probably as old as he is. If we logically deduce it now, I don't think he has the necessary cash.« Diyar replied.

»Come to think of it, that makes sense.« Nabih responded with a lowered head.

»Do you remember back when we used to play not far from the abandoned military base?« Diyar asked.

»Yes, of course, Bennou was stationed there for several years. I can still vividly remember the roar when we watched the fighter jets take off from close by, soaring steeply into the sky after liftoff. Imagine, we could hijack one of those elegant machines and fly over all our problems at supersonic speed.« Nabih reminisced.

»If those old relics weren't already rusting away for decades, maybe. But it's not as easy as in your imagination. However, there might be something there that we can call our own soon. So you won't be left alone.«

»Your plans always sound so darn simple in theory. And then I'm left high and dry once it gets down to the nitty-gritty.« Nabih remarked.

»Interesting, from my recollection, a few

hours ago, I was the one standing there looking foolish. Or am I mistaken?« Diyar retorted.

»No, no. You're absolutely right. But then again, you were the first one to crawl out of the pit with your hands raised.« Nabih conceded.

»Yes, and what do you think I should've done? Those crazy eyes, the mystery surrounding his Nazi past didn't exactly contribute to relaxation. None of us could have guessed that Monsieur Friedrich is actually a kind-hearted person.« Diyar explained.

»Well, he's not exactly a saint. Otherwise, he would have obliterated his comrades right after the murder of the nomad.« Nabih recalled.

»Whatever the case, I'm just glad we're both still alive. What's done is done. We can't undo it, unfortunately.« Nabih nodded with a smile and swiftly brought up the next question.

»How on earth did you plan to overcome the barbed wire fence and get past the guards with the dogs?«

»You mean the one-eyed blind man who sits in the sun all day with his lapdog. Ridiculous, he won't notice us at all?«

»Are you sure it's just one guard and one dog? I remember it differently somehow.«

»Stop worrying unnecessarily. Yesterday, we did it your way, and tomorrow, we'll play by my rules. It'll be a piece of cake.«

»If that were true, I wouldn't be freaking out already.«

»Of course, there's some risk involved. But that's what makes it exciting. Do you think the Egyptian pyramids would exist if everything had always been easy?«

»Normally, I'm up for any fun. But right

now, I feel like the pilot trying to prevent his plane from crashing. However, my inner panic is so great that my actions are without any structure, and I'm gradually succumbing to my fear.«

»No way. No plane will ever crash as long as I'm the co-pilot. And no friend will ever be left behind with their worries. Once you've internalized that, we'll meet tomorrow at sunset at the same spot where we used to watch the machines.«

»Got it! But why the sudden rush?«

»I urgently need to visit my grandpa again. See you tomorrow.« As Nabih was left behind with a puzzled expression, Diyar marched quickly toward the east. Outside the house, he encountered Bennou, who managed to greet him before his grandson started blabbering.

»Grandpa, we now know who Monsieur Friedrich really is.«

»A hello or good evening would have been a better start for me. But today's youth isn't what it used to be. Why are you so dirty anyway? Were you playing with your friend in the sand again?«

»Something like that. We were on another exploration tour and found some interesting things.«

»That doesn't sound like the original plan. Weren't you supposed to visit him at his shop?«

»We did. But then everything changed. The pottery shard is practically worthless, just as you suspected. But what's more interesting is the fact that Friedrich has been one of us for years, even though he used to be a Nazi. But...« Bennou interrupted his grandson loudly, shaking his head disdainfully.

»I knew it. My intuition has never failed me.«

»Now, let me finish, I wasn't done yet.«

»Sorry, please continue.«

»After the murder of a Bedouin committed by his comrades, he switched sides. He talked about pain, guilt that haunted him and ultimately made him a better person. During his narration, you could clearly see from his expression that he was ashamed of his past and wanted nothing to do with the crimes under the swastika.«

»That may all be true. But internalize this. The truth in the end is always just the sum of what you tell and what people believe. That's why I would always be cautious about what complete strangers serve up to me.«

»Oh, Grandpa, I knew from the start that you're skeptical. That's why I arranged a meeting where you two can exchange thoughts. You should visit him at his shop whenever you have time.«

»You and your odd ideas. I'll gladly accept the meeting, but not because I want to judge him, but because I believe everyone has the right to be heard. Besides all the news, I can't shake the feeling that you still have something on your mind. I can see it in the unrest in your eyes.« Diyar knew his grandpa's keen insight and spoke openly.

»Nabih and I were planning to visit your old military base tomorrow evening.«

»And that's why you had such a gloomy face.«

»Yes, because I thought you would forbid

it.«

»Even if I did, would you have listened to me? Or would you have disobeyed my order? Be honest.«

»Probably, I would have gone anyway.«

»That's why prohibitions are complete nonsense because they always lead to lies. But one question, I do have. What exactly are you two up to? Don't tell me you're going on a treasure hunt again.«

»Something like that.« Diyar grinned mischievously.

»You don't have to tell me any details, that's enough. But be careful, there are things there not meant for your eyes. Now, hurry up so Karim and Mum can sleep peacefully. I don't want them blaming me for your tardiness in the end.« After a brief hug, Diyar headed straight to his parents' house, with the feeling that Bennou was up to something. The next day, Nabih arrived at the agreed meeting point just before sunset. Nervously, he paced back and forth, observing the surroundings through the fence. From a distance, he could see the lined-up fighter jets, which immediately captivated him with their sheer presence. Just as he heard the distant barking of dogs, Diyar sneaked up from behind and whispered into his ear.

»Hands up, you old rascal.« Nabih turned around laughing and looked bewildered at the shovel his friend immediately began to dig a hole with.

»Hey, why don't we just climb over instead of digging through the sand like earthworms?«

»With your glasses, you look like a mole, but the clever one between us seems to be me.

If we climb over, we'll land right on the silver platter. But if we crawl under the fence, we're practically invisible.«

»But you said there's only the one-eyed blind man with his lapdog wandering around the premises. So, I wonder why you're making such an effort here?« Annoyed, Diyar waved him off and continued to shovel diligently. Meanwhile, Nabih sneaked away and shortly after called out loudly from the other side of the fence,

»The mole made it over, you wise guy!« Completely perplexed, his buddy looked up and, with shovel in hand, crossed over as well. Not five meters further, they faced a growling guard dog, baring its teeth and blocking their path.

»Saints preserve us, so this is what your lapdog

looks like.« while panic was written all over Nabih's face.

»If we had crawled underneath, the beast wouldn't have noticed us at all. So stop blaming me.« Diyar retorted

»The blame game won't be necessary soon, because this fellow here will tear the flesh off our bones in no time.« Nabih grimly remarked.

»Wait, I have an idea.«

»Come on, hurry up, I don't want to offer my entrails to the vultures.« Diyar urged.

»Slowly raise your arms, walk backward, and avoid any eye contact.« Nabih instructed. Before he could receive a response, Diyar panicked and sprinted towards the runway, with the dog barking in pursuit. Nabih watched astonished as a dust cloud abruptly ended in front of one of the fighter jets, over whose wing his friend managed to secure himself in the nick of time. Completely out of breath, Diyar collapsed to the ground and looked down in amazement at Nabih, who knocked out the aggressive four-legged creature with the shovel. "That wasn't exactly the most graceful exit. Do you think it's still alive?«

»Why don't you jump down, you coward, and then you can give it CPR to bring it back from the dead?«

»Yeah, okay, I left you hanging. But that's no reason to hold a grudge permanently. After all, we're best friends?«

»I'm not holding a grudge. But a true friend would have at least gotten bitten. Now, come on, or do you want to linger up there until late at night?" In one swift move, Diyar descended and headed straight for an abandoned building, through an open window they gained entry. Inside, an eerie silence prevailed, interrupted only by the rustling of the wind carrying desert sand.

»Have you actually thought about what we're doing here?«

»No, have you? I'm letting my instincts guide me. Look around, there must be something here that we can turn into money.« Cautiously, they took one step after another until Nabih excitedly called out to his friend. With wide eyes, they stood in front of a dusty desk, upon which lay a stack of files, military orders, and an old map. With unease, Diyar leaned over and pointed with his finger at the circled areas, which furrowed his brow with worry.

»Do you think what I'm thinking?«

»Of course! In the northeast, persecuted

minorities in our country live. That's where my grandparents come from. If my instincts are correct, they ordered the attacks on the remote mountain regions from here. That was the chemical attack where more than five thousand people died.« When Bassem heard this, he sighed in horror, and the blood in his veins froze. Sitting there as if petrified, he let his lips speak while his mind was elsewhere.

»Son, I'm terribly sorry to interrupt you. But the terrible events of the past suddenly re-surface. All that despair, the cries, and that un-speakable helplessness, enveloped in the scent of sweet apples, are hard to bear. But the beauty of it is that, for a fraction of a second in my memory, my sons were alive again.« With great empathy, Amira and Zainab comforted him, while Diyar gradually continued his narrative.

»I had no idea about any of this.«

»About the gas attack?«

»No, that your parents come from the same region.«

»That's completely irrelevant now. Look into the files instead, maybe there's something important in there.« Page by page, Diyar flipped through the documents until he came across several delivery notes from foreign companies.

»Here are the names of three German companies that supplied the precursor chemicals for the production of chemical weapons. They're all labeled as herbicides.« Diyar explained.

»Probably because they wanted to disguise what this devil's brew was actually intended for.« Nabih added solemnly.

»And our countrymen then mixed the substances in the factories and unleashed the demon of cruelty from the bottle.«

»Exactly. But what shocks me the most is the fact that there wasn't a big outcry in Europe.«

»Maybe nobody knew about it?«

»You don't believe that yourself. Nowadays, they know before you even go to the toilet that you're going to the toilet. So, don't tell me fairy tales. The West didn't want blood on their hands. Otherwise, they would have delivered it through official channels.«

»And what do we do with this information now?«

»It's obvious. We take the documents with us and, after our escape, we'll let the world know the truth.«

»I'm not sure if that's such a good idea.«

»Well, to me, it sounds like an excellent idea. Maybe we'll even be awarded the Nobel Peace Prize.«

»Do as you please.« Nabih silently pocketed the documents while Diyar went over to the control panel and randomly pressed a few buttons. Seconds later, a sliding gate opened with a loud squeak, leading into a hangar. Without hesitation, they stepped into the darkness, which filled Nabih with fear.

»When I saw you fiddling with the buttons, I got really nervous. Couldn't you have pressed another button so we wouldn't be stumbling around in the dark like blind men?«

»Instead of whining like a little child, you could have turned on the light switch ages ago. Move aside, I'll take care of it for you.« One by one, the fluorescent tubes flickered on, illuminating the room with a buzzing sound. With mouths agape, they looked up at a black supersonic aircraft surrounded by stacked wooden crates.

»Goodness gracious. Do you think this thing was stolen? Bennou warned me that there are things here not meant for our eyes.«

»I don't think so. But I can't help but wonder again why you can't keep your mouth shut for once in your life.«

»I wonder the same about you.«

»It's innate in me. But with you, it's pure intent.« Nabih quipped, punctuating his statement with a broad grin.

»Calm down, or do you think Grandpa is going to send a lightning bolt down from above onto our heads?«

»You never know with him, his aura has something supernatural.« As they conversed, both approached the crates, which they pried open with a metal rod. In the first ones, they found machine guns from Russia. In the subsequent ones, they found missiles from France, as well as hundreds of rocket-propelled grenades from China.

»Hey Diyar, you know what's sad about our discovery?«

»That we haven't found anything yet that we can turn into money?«

»No, that's not what I meant. Look around you. Everything around us is designed to destroy people. People who look like you and me. The major powers talk publicly about peace while exporting suffering and misery behind the scenes. Dictatorial regimes arm themselves to the teeth with weapons bought abroad, ensuring their survival for decades. And as long as money flows, no one will ever question their actions. Unless someone becomes too powerful, then the West ensures they quickly disappear into obscurity with a coup. We are just the beginning. The strong leaders in the Middle East are becoming fewer and the refugee flows are rapidly increasing.«

»My family has told me quite a bit about the world, but your knowledge exceeds the norm again. Did you read about this or how do you know all of this?«

»Oh, I've picked up bits and pieces here and there. Come on, grab one of those rifles and let's get out of here. I just heard a faint barking.« They hastily made their way toward the exit, where they saw the canine sniffing in their direction through the window.

»Darn it, your striking power can't be relied on anymore.«

»What are you talking about? I hit it with full force.«

»Apparently not, otherwise the fatso wouldn't be heading straight for us.«

»Nobody can help it if your lapdog has nine lives.«

»Alright, let me show you how it's done.« With a swift motion, Diyar unlocked the rifle and fired several shots towards the dog. But it dodged in zigzag motions and leaped through the open window, biting Nabih's shoulder in mid-air. Diyar reacted immediately, striking the furry attacker's skull with the butt of the rifle so hard that it fell to the ground motionless.

»Phew, that was damn close. Where did

you learn to shoot? From the one-eyed blind man?«

»How about a thank you. Because if I hadn't reacted, that little nip would've turned into a big mess.«

»Little nip? I was seriously injured just now. You need to get help urgently.«

»Your noggin is still intact, so there's no need to panic. Besides, I don't see any blood anywhere, just a whining mutt feeling sorry for itself.«

»Ouch, I'd love to punch you right now.«

»See, as long as you're still in attack mode, everything's fine. I'm out. Would you like to come along?«

»You're asking that now?« As they stepped out, several bursts of machine gun fire flew past them, driving them back inside. Nabih climbed into the cockpit of the fighter jet as if in a trance, followed by his friend. Huddled together, they sat in the transparent canopy, whispering as they observed their surroundings.

»Interesting how a seriously injured person manages to climb up the wings of a fighter jet. By the way, the story smelled just as fishy as the one about the one-legged beggar who supposedly chased you at night and wanted to beat the life out of you for no reason.«

»As if you've never fibbed before.«

»Well, yes, I have. But unlike you, I don't make a mountain out of a molehill.« Simultaneously, three heavily armed men entered the hangar, quickly splitting up and cautiously inspecting every corner.

»Come on, Diyar, do something!«

»Yeah, and what?«

»I don't know. But once they realize the rifles are missing, they'll turn us into Swiss cheese. Here, take the documents, they're safer with you.«

»Why me?«

»Just do as I say and press a few buttons, it worked just now.« Just as Diyar raised his posterior and tucked the documents into his back pocket, one of the soldiers spotted his head. With a hand signal, he alerted his comrades, who quickly surrounded him and loudly demanded that he come down. But when nothing happened, one of the men lost patience and fired several shots in his direction. In panic, Nabih pressed all the buttons, causing the black bomb attached beneath the aircraft to detach. With a loud scream of terror, all the soldiers dropped to the ground and watched with bated breath as the bomb rolled past them sideways, hitting the wooden crates a few seconds later without detonating. A relieved sigh filled the room, and the two of them dashed out into the pitch-black night in a desperate act of determination. Bullets whizzed past them as Nabih suddenly tumbled down into an air duct. Without hesitation, Diyar jumped in right after him. Completely disoriented, they crawled through the extensive ducts while the soldiers in the background could be heard threateningly.

Finally, they reached a large underground facility equipped with dozens of monitors and futuristic-looking devices.

»What's this place?« Nabih looked around questioningly, brushing the sand off his shoulder.

»No idea, but judging by the way they fired at us up there, I don't think anyone else should ever see this place.«

»Do me a favor and don't touch anything. We don't want to start World War III from down here.«

»You're probably still in shock, otherwise you would have noticed that you were the one who knocked the bomb off the plane.«

»But that doesn't mean you should go touching everything with your grubby hands.«

»Don't worry. I'm just blowing the dust off the switches so I can see what's written on them.« At that moment, Nabih shouted loudly, pointing at dozens of explosive devices loaded with chemical warfare agents Sarin, Tabun, and mustard gas from Germany.

»Man, why are you shouting? Did you just see God himself?«

»No, but Satan. Look over there. Those are the terrible things they dropped on our innocent brothers and sisters.«

»Are you sure?«

»Hell yes. Look at the numbers on those inconspicuous dark barrels over there, and compare them to the numbers on the delivery notes.« Full of curiosity, Diyar went over and, after a quick inspection, looked horrified.

»You were right. Do you know where we are?«

»If I'm not mistaken, we're right in the factory. This is where they put together their explosive devices from the raw materials.«

»Yes, but seeing it with my own eyes gives the horror a face. A face I never thought actually existed.«

»Believe me, the goosebumps this sight gives me can't be described in words. Do you see any way out of here without getting caught? Because I just heard voices.« Hastily, they wandered from door to door, only one of which would open. They ran through it quickly, the monotonous sound of their footsteps drowned out by the approaching echo of heavy boots. Panting, they stopped and hid in a dark corner, frantically discussing their next move.

»Hey, do you still have the documents in your pocket?«

»Of course.« replied Diyar firmly.

»From here on, our adventure is coming to an end.«

»What nonsense are you babbling about now?«

»Didn't you hear the footsteps? They've surrounded us, we can't go forward or backward.«

»Just standing around won't get us anywhere, so pull yourself together and stay close behind me.« Noticeably hesitant, Nabih complied with the request and followed his friend to the exit, where they counted slowly to three. With eyes closed, they opened the gate and immediately faced the barrels of several machine guns aimed directly at them. They turned to the side with raised hands, where to their surprise, Bennou and Monsieur Friedrich appeared, conversing with the officer of the soldiers.

»Today is our lucky day. We're free faster than you can count to three.« But Nabih kept his response to himself and was taken away at that moment. Anxiously, Diyar watched his friend being led away, who turned around one last time, smiling and waving at him, just like he did back on the school path.

The Price of Freedom

All were torn by the story and engaged in lively conversation. Eventually, Amira and Zainab turned to Diyar, who had no idea what was happening as questions bombarded him one after another.

»What happened next? What about Nabih? Did you see him again? How did it happen that Grandpa Bennou and Monsieur Friedrich showed up together at the scene? Did they reconcile? And where are the documents you took from the military base?« When no response came, Bassem intervened with his calmness, trying to calm down the curious minds.

»How about letting the poor boy catch his breath before bombarding him with hundreds of questions.« Everyone looked ashamed and apologized for their intrusiveness, prompting the helmsman to interject abruptly.

»You're quite a bunch. On one hand, I've made hundreds of crossings, but stories like these have never come my way. I shouldn't feel any sympathy, but your tales are so moving that it gets to me. That's never happened before.« For a brief moment, there was absolute silence before the confused pantsless man cheekily spoke up.

»Perhaps you're finally becoming human and not a heartless robot like Ibrahim and Omar, those greedy bastards.« When he noticed that his statement didn't resonate with his fellow sufferers, he realized he had gone a bit too far with his remark.

»It's extremely interesting that those who can least afford it are the ones who talk the most. If I were Ibrahim, I would have left you to the sharks after what you did with Amira. In my eyes, Omar is actually an honorable man, whose four-letter name I never want to hear from your foul mouth again. Did that sink in? I'll take your strange nod as a yes. What's your name, by the way? Just in case we have to write a farewell letter to your family in the near future.«

»Abdul« came out meekly from him.

»Louder, my ears aren't what they used to be.«

»My name is Abdul, sir.«

»That's better. You seem to possess some usable manners after all. That still doesn't justify that stupid grin. Sit back down before I lose my temper and do something I might regret later. Where were we?«

No one dared to make a sound. Everyone knew that the stout man at the helm was a powder keg that could explode at any moment with a wrong remark.

»Oh, come on, don't look at me so frightened. Did you seriously think I'd abandon our big mouth to his fate? He's way too precious for that. It was all just a joke. Right, Abdul? Abdul?«

»Yeah, right« he replied, head lowered.

»Well, I don't want to be a spoilsport just because some don't know how to behave. Better make sure to quiet your kids with the cookies, lest I get some foolish ideas.« he said, laughing paranoidly. They passed the packages without a murmur until someone unexpectedly stood up and pointed to the distant lights.

»There's land over there. We must be really

close.« The man at the helm immediately interrupted and brought everyone back down to earth with his statement.

»Yes, very close to misery. Because what you see twinkling there isn't Western Europe, but North Africa. The coast guard doesn't treat strangers like us very kindly, so we have to be extremely careful not to be discovered.«

»Really? Who told you such nonsense?« came the incredulous reply.

»Unbelievable, do we still have such a skeptic on board who thinks he knows better? You can swim over there and see for yourself if you doubt my statement. But don't say I didn't warn you.« While the doubter pondered a response, two headlights suddenly lit up from the darkness, then immediately went out after a brief sweep. Everyone on board was equally surprised by the action and called out multiple times toward the ship, thinking they were on the brink of rescue. But this turned out to be a fatal misconception when, without warning, gunfire erupted.

With full force, they sped away over the waves. Panicked cries rang out, drowning out the bursts of machine gun fire piercing through the wooden hull. After over an hour, they reached international waters. There, they breathed a sigh of relief and plugged the leaks that were letting water slowly seep inside. Everyone pitched in until the boat was dry enough to resume their journey.

»Well, you skeptic, you don't need to hide behind the children. I hope my answer satisfies you.« the helmsman said angrily toward the skeptic.

»I'm terribly sorry for doubting. In my wildest nightmares, I never would have thought they'd shoot at us, especially when we're in distress.« the skeptic replied humbly.

»Oh, that's nothing new. I could tell you much worse stories. They can do as they please in their territorial waters. They could have sunk us deliberately, but they want us to go back out to sea and not die right on their doorstep. After a hearty breakfast in the sun, no vacationer wants to scrape dead refugees off the beach.«

»That's so sick.«

»Maybe to you. But my thought isn't far-fetched. The problem is getting out of hand. The neighboring countries are overwhelmed by the situation because everyone is left to fend for themselves. There's anarchy, no structure, and the fight is being waged on the backs of the poorest, who desperately sail around the world's oceans in their nutshell boats, hoping in vain for help.«

»Hasn't anyone ever reported on this?«

»Not that I know of. It would reveal that the West is to blame for the whole dilemma. Or do you think people leave their homes because they're so happy there? Bassem was right about what he said earlier. Politics, with their arms deliveries to unstable systems, have brought forth future flashpoints just to get their hands on black gold as cheaply as possible. They may have driven their economy forward, but at the same time, they've fed the devil who, in his megalomania, will one day lash out blindly. This has set in motion a fatal process in the surrounding countries that couldn't be stopped. If I were young again, I'd act just like you. I'd grab my family and get out of the way of the spewing volcano that robs you of your future with its molten lava. Instead of staring at me in amazement, why don't you tell me your name, mustachioed skeptic?«

»Can we stick to my nickname for now? I need some time to process all this. It's a lot for me right now.«

»Sure, no problem. But don't drive yourself crazy and look forward. The chaos was already here before you were born. My generation at least enjoyed a glimmer of prosperity, but it looks very bleak for you poor souls. I think you've got enough food for thought to chew on until we arrive.«

»If we even make it there.« came the whispering reply.

»I missed that entirely. Diyar, my friend!«

the helmsman roared with the volume of a megaphone from one side to the other.

»How long were you planning to keep us on tenterhooks? You can entertain yourself with Amira, Zainab, and Bassem for quite a while. And little Adil can certainly occupy himself for a bit too.«

»That wasn't my intention, I apologize. But after the attack, I just couldn't bring myself to it. Where should I start?«

»Well, logically, where your narrative left off.«

»Right, now I remember.« After Nabih was taken into custody, Grandpa grabbed my arm roughly and lectured me, as I was about to break free.

»Don't be foolish. If you don't listen to me, you'll harm your friend more than you'll help him. Most likely, you'll see him again in a few weeks.«

»But then it will be too late.« he spoke utterly dejectedly to himself. At a walking pace, the soldiers escorted us outside, where they saluted farewell before returning to their posts. Amidst all the turmoil in his mind, Diyar realized with horror that his grandpa had eventually shown up with the man he couldn't stand at the scene. He kept looking to the left and pinched his thigh because he simply couldn't believe what he was seeing.

»Bennou, if your grandson keeps looking to the side, he'll get a stiff neck. Can we afford that?«

»I think so. My grandson can take a lot, he's tough.«

»Yes, I've already had a taste of that. I've

never met anyone in my life who digs holes faster than he can fill them.«

»It runs in the family, my son was also of that sort.« Completely baffled, Diyar stared over and stuttered from one question to the next.

»How on earth? When on earth? Where on earth?«

»If I recall correctly, it was all your idea. Now we're here together, and you're still not satisfied.«

»I only made up the meeting because I thought you wouldn't show up anyway.«

»Leopold, today's youth is completely confused. They say one thing and mean something completely different. At our age, you just can't keep up.«

»Leopold? You even address each other by

your first names?«

»Son, we're entitled to it, after all, we're from the same year.«

»How is it that you get along so well? I think I'm dreaming.«

»Bennou, feel free, I trust you completely.« nodded Friedrich relaxedly.

»It's actually quite simple. The hatred I felt towards a stranger was externally ignited. All the dislike formed from what I heard and what I was internally convinced of.«

»Yes, and how did you tear down this old thought construct?«

»I opened my heart and no longer allowed my prejudice to determine my thinking and thus my actions.«

»Grandpa, that's fascinating. I'm terribly sorry for reacting so disrespectfully. But I would have never thought all this was possible.«

»That's perfectly understandable. After all, you carry around a backpack of prejudices through which you view the world. Let it all sink in at the right time, it will free you.«

»I will. What do we do now with Nabih? We can't allow them to imprison him innocently.«

»They won't. At the moment, they need every man they can get. My fear is that after two weeks in custody, they'll send him directly to the front.«

»To the front? That means certain death. Why did you allow them to take him with them?« Diyar's facial expressions slipped away.

»We didn't, trust me. I used my good contacts, and Leopold traded his entire inventory so they wouldn't lock you up. Our hands were literally tied.«

»My boat is leaving the harbor in less than a week. There must be some way to free him. Otherwise, I see myself forced to stay here.« Diyar waited anxiously for a response, his gaze inevitably falling on Monsieur Friedrich, who joined the discussion.

»Setting aside the fact that I wasn't particularly attached to my accumulated possessions, there is always a way. However hopeless it may seem. Before we arrived with our company in this dreamy desert region, we crossed a mountain range in northern Italy with trucks and dozens of supply vehicles. At a pass not far from Gran Paradiso, we fell into an ambush that almost cost me my life. We couldn't comprehend the world anymore because we thought our countries were allies and we enjoyed high esteem among the population. Behind almost every corner, partisans lurked, just waiting to send us to hell. They impaled the decapitated heads of murdered Nazis on wooden stakes, positioning them right next to the town entrance sign.

Over time, we became so paranoid that for every necessity within the company, a squad of ten would always go out to secure the immediate surroundings. We still had almost two thousand kilometers to go to the ferry in the south of the country. Although the war was still an eternity away, each of us felt that we were marching towards it in giant strides. One evening, we stopped in a small community, where my officer gathered us in the church. He seemed agitated and reported heavy losses that the company ahead of us had to endure. Internally, the rumor of a defector, originally named Rudolf Jacobs and known by his combat name 'Comandante Rodolfo', circulated, causing fear and terror among his former comrades. This news shook us all, as Jacobs was considered absolutely loyal within the army. At that time, we weren't battle-tested yet, but our self-confidence and eagerness were so immense that we didn't see the renegade defector as a real problem.

However, our officer had a completely different opinion and changed his original plan, which is why he initiated 'Operation Octopus' that very night. We all looked at him quite puzzled because nobody could imagine anything under that term. Gradually, however, he shed light on the matter and explained what we had to do.

The three most important individuals, including myself, were to disguise themselves as tourists and scout the routes ahead of us. Their main task was to locate partisan hideouts and unveil the secret surrounding 'Comandante Rodolfo'. So it happened that the next day, in a vehicle of Italian make, we drove along the serpentine roads, while our company stayed behind in the village awaiting our clearance.

Diyar was eventually so enthusiastic that it bubbled out of him.

»That's extremely clever. If it were up to me, I'd dress up like a Mafioso today and get started.«

»Before you recklessly plunge into misfortune, you need to know where or how to start.«

Bennou cautioned him to be careful.

»It's quite simple. One of us goes out as a scout and locates Nabih. The others wait in the background for the order and move in for the rescue. That's why it's called 'Operation Octopus'. Because these creatures perfectly blend into their surroundings and outsmart their opponents with their intelligence.«

»Really? Was that also your officer's main idea? Or is my grandson just making up some fairy tale?«

»I don't mean to contradict you. But I'm afraid he's right. Just with the difference that today we're using our intellect instead of a weapon.«

»Wait a minute, did you intend to put yourself in such danger in your old age? After all, I'm the one who dragged you into this mess.«

»I may have gathered a bit of dust, but I've been eagerly anticipating such an exciting adventure for years. I can still guard the furniture in my modest four walls even if I'm in a wheelchair. Besides, I didn't exactly participate unwillingly in your grandson's rescue. I haven't felt this alive in ages. Do you perhaps have an idea where Nabih could be?«

»If my guess is correct, they've taken him to the police station at the old bridge. That's how they used to handle it in my time, and I don't think that's changed. He could be somewhere else, but I doubt it.« Diyar followed the conversation with great excitement as the two went over every tiny detail.

At dawn the next day, Bennou and his grandson stood disguised as fishermen on the bridge, with a direct view of the police station. In the lantern light, Monsieur Friedrich could be seen entering the building after tying his shoes.

»That was the signal. From now on, all we can do is hope.«

»Why so pessimistic? Do you know something I don't?«

»I don't think so.« Diyar stuttered nervously.

»Come on, spill the beans before I get uncomfortable.«

»Did he tell you about the gun, by the way?«

»Heavens, now it all makes sense. That's why he was so distant this morning. I was wondering why he was acting so strangely. He didn't want me to pick him up, nor did he want to be hugged when we greeted each other. I don't know what he's up to, but my gut feeling doesn't bode well.«

»But you've been wrong about that many times before.«

»This is completely different now.«

»I don't think he'd jeopardize the entire operation with a reckless move. He's far too intelligent for that.«

»Be cautious, it's precisely these individuals who end up plunging everyone else into misfortune because they think they know and can do everything.«

»The more we talk about it, the more uneasy I feel. Do you even believe that Nabih is being held at the police station?«

»I can't say with one hundred percent certainty. But since you've been snooping around like strays, I think they'll question him first before locking him up. And I hope you haven't seen anything that wasn't meant for your eyes. If you did, pray that he keeps quiet. Because spies aren't particularly favored by the regime.« Diyar continued to ponder inwardly and eventually pulled out the documents he had pocketed the previous day.

»Grandpa, I have to confess something.«

»Please don't, that's never the start of a good story.«

»Well, we only went to the military base to steal something we could sell. But all we found were weapons, ammunition, and planes that are difficult, if not impossible, to sell.«

»What did you expect to find there? It was clear from the beginning that you wouldn't be roaring down the runway in a fighter jet or driving off the lot in a tank. Say no more, what interests me much more is what's up with those damn documents you're tremblingly holding out to me.« With a deliberate gaze, Bennou scanned the papers, which, the longer he looked at them, visibly made him shudder.

»If someone catches wind of what we have here, we'll be in big trouble. Oh, who am I kidding, if anyone finds out, we'll be just as dead as the poor souls on whom they dropped this stuff. Did that escape your youthful recklessness?«

»Well, I knew it was sensitive material. But I didn't think we could be sentenced to death because of it. I wanted to take the documents to Europe so I could present them to the public.«

»And how long do you think it would have taken for them to find out who stole them?« his grandfather spoke angrily through clenched teeth.

»No idea, maybe ten years.«

»Once again, it shows that you have neither life experience nor foresight. Secret agents equipped with the latest technology are everywhere. It wouldn't take five minutes for them to catch you.«

»Probably, they already have us on their radar.«

»To be honest, I don't want to find out, so I'll destroy the papers on the spot.« Internally, Diyar flinched as he saw the flaming match igniting the papers.

»I know what you're thinking, but with your recklessness, you would have put all our lives at risk, and I can't allow that.« Suddenly, screams could be heard from a distance. People panicked, leaving the police station, among them Nabih and Monsieur Friedrich, who had taken a hostage, pressing a gun against his temple. Diyar's heart raced. He fixated on his friend, who stood frozen, not moving an inch. Without the situation appearing to escalate, a man from the ambush suddenly opened fire. Bloodied, the hostage-taker collapsed, while Nabih managed to escape unnoticed.

»Let's get out of here quickly, there's nothing more we can do for him.« Bennou shook his head in dismay.

»But you can't just leave him like that. After what he's done for us.«

»He made his decision. That was the price of freedom, and we have to accept it. Now come on.« An hour later, they arrived at the agreed meeting point outside the city.

Despite the reunion of the two friends, the mood was somber. Together, they paid their respects to Leopold Friedrich and laid the identification tag exactly where his fallen comrades were buried.

Spring of Hope

Like pulled by an invisible string, the boat sliced through the calm sea. It was a starry night. Zainab and the others were sound asleep. Quietly, little Adil sneaked away and headed straight for Diyar, who was dozing off.

»Wake up, wake up.« he shook his arm.

»What's wrong? Why aren't you with your mother?« his counterpart rubbed his eyes, startled.

»You see, I'm already big. That's why I don't have to sleep.«

»But you must be tired, right?«

»That's what Mum always says. But here, there are only sad people, so I stay awake for a long time so I don't dream about it.«

»What made you sad?«

»Well, you and your friend Bih.«

»You mean Nabih.«

»Exactly. Why isn't he here?« the little one looked at him impatiently.

»Because he has to work a lot at home. When I see him, I'll tell him that I met a new friend named Adil who's already big.«

»Oh yes! And will you also tell him that I want a train and lots of toys? He can play too. Before, Baba used to do that, but he's not here anymore.«

»Where is he?«

»Mum says he's with the angels.« Suddenly, Diyar was speechless. He looked pleadingly at Zainab, who, with tears in her eyes, held her child close and returned to her place. Meanwhile, the helmsman waved him over. After a brief instruction, he handed the helm to

Diyar and hurried to the bow, where he relieved himself before returning relieved.

»I hope you focused on the compass and didn't maneuver us into the next disaster. Our boat can withstand an attack. But at the next one, we'll likely have to swim to shore.«

»What difference does it make?«

»Is everything okay with you? I haven't seen you this discouraged since we left the port.«

»Not at all. If everything were fine, I wouldn't be cramped up on this tiny nutshell waiting for my end.«

»I can understand your thoughts, but I still find it unacceptable how hard you are on yourself. Your friend was denied the opportunity to escape. And I believe he would have given his last shirt just to be by your side. So, I advise you to face your fate with a little more respect. After all, you're still alive.«

»But you have no idea what has happened to Nabih.«

»No, but I can read between the lines. Nothing that happens on board escapes me.«
Visibly dejected, Diyar sat on the floor, hiding his face with his hands as he spoke.

»You talk about fate and respect. But you're not in my situation, so how can you even remotely understand how I think or what I feel?«

»No one I've ever transported was exactly like you. But still, you're very similar. Whether poor, rich, young, or old. What unites all of you is your fear.«

»Fear?«

»Yes, it has slowly spread and is now omnipresent. Haven't you noticed?«

»Now that you mention it, I feel it more consciously.«

»I still remember your hopeful look when you boarded. There's hardly any of that left in you or the others. Except for the children, for whom all this seems to be a great adventure.«

»Can I be honest?«

»Nothing would please me more.«

»At first, your intimidating appearance and fiery temper didn't really sit well with me. But you seem like a nice guy, whose name no one knows.«

»Actually, I pulled Amira out of the waves and saved our confused, pants-less big mouth Abdul from a draconian punishment. That alone should have answered your questions. Just call me Rubi. That's what everyone who knows me calls me.«

»Sounds interesting! Where in the world do you come from?«

»I'm not from that far away. I was born in the neighboring country. I lived there with my family and my sister until I was nine years old, but unfortunately, she's no longer with us.«

»Oh, my condolences. That must be very painful.«

»Thank you, but it's okay. The grief has long passed, but the memory is still present. Especially on days like these.«

»Why? What's the significance?«

»Alright, I'll tell you, but promise me you'll remain calm while I do. I don't want the others to think I'm weak.«

»Of course! It would be an honor to listen to you.«

»Whenever winter bid farewell and the

scent of impending spring arrived, my sister and I would rush out of the house. With over-whelming joy, we'd frolic in the meadow until we collapsed from exhaustion. Then, we'd just lie there, counting the blades of grass and wax-ing lyrical about Mum's delicious Tajines, which she prepared with so much love. Late in the evening, our father would come home, al-ways eating first before tucking us into bed. We'd make fun of his dark appearance, which he got from working in a mine nearby. Until that moment, we were a normal family living in a neighborhood where all the children came from working-class parents. We were grateful for what we had and didn't care about what happened outside our little world. But this little world collapsed like a house of cards on that spring day.

Dreamily, I walked home from school, passing countless buses filled with people from my neighborhood. I immediately recognized my friend's uncle, who didn't react to my wave but instead stared lifelessly through me. In front of our apartment building, two grim-looking soldiers with their machine guns pointed the way to the bus for my family. The only thing we were allowed to take was what we wore. A silent helplessness engulfed us, even immobilizing my father, who always had a solution for everything. None of us knew what was happening or had the slightest idea of what awaited us. Every attempt to communicate with the driver or a fellow passenger was met with a terse, 'Quiet, you'll see.' It wasn't until nightfall when everyone was asleep that I overheard a conversation my mother was having in hushed tones with an unknown woman.

»Where are they taking us? Are we going to some camp to be exterminated?«

»I've heard they're resettling us in the border area.«

»But why? We haven't done anything wrong.«

»I know. But in times like these, we're like commodities.«

»What do you mean?«

»Refugees are being used as bargaining chips nowadays. Anyone who doesn't make it to Europe is worth a lot of money.«

»I'm sorry, you're speaking in riddles. I understand absolutely nothing of what you're telling me.«

»Let me put it this way. We're the leverage

so that our country can extort billions from Western governments. In return, our politicians keep the borders closed and ensure that our European neighbors aren't flooded with streams of refugees.«

»Yes, and what can we do about it?«

»Nothing, but we belong to a minority that has no rights. With us, they can do whatever they want. History has shown that abundantly.«

»Someone has to come to our aid.«

»No one from outside will intervene. Especially not when it ensures stability in their own country.«

»These people are beyond help. I need to digest this before I can comprehend it.«

»It won't change anything. A man told me that many countries are following our example because the business is extremely lucrative. From now on, we're just spectators, decisions will be made over our heads, as banal as it may sound.«

»And how long do we have to stay where we're going? My husband has heart problems, and my children need to go to school.«

»No one knows for sure. Sometimes a few hundred are allowed through and then they're allowed to walk on foot.«

»Back home?«

»No, no. To a foreign country. The home we knew exists only in our memories now. The apartment, as well as personal belongings, have long been handed over to their countrymen.«

»That's inhumane and degrading.«

»I know. We could revolt, but being a hostage is still better than being killed.«

»Not for me.« she replied in a subdued voice, looking at the soldier dozing off in front of her.

Several hours passed until we came to a stop in the early morning at the border area. My father pulled me out of the bus, still half asleep, and my sister followed. Before joining the procession, we stared in disbelief down into the valley. Before our eyes, a gigantic tent city was erected, surrounded by fences, looking like a huge prison under the open sky. Even though no one spoke, I could feel the pain spreading across my parents' faces. The first night, we spent outdoors because there was chaos and no one felt responsible for us. There was no electricity, no running water, and the sanitary facilities were holes dug into the desert sand by people's bare hands.

We encountered people who had fled their home countries because of the war. And there we were, right in the middle of it all. A displaced family reduced to pawns in a political game due to our ethnic minority status. My parents marriage suffered greatly from the situation. My mother relatively quickly adapted to her new surroundings. She made friends, took loving care of us, and halved her daily food rations so we wouldn't go hungry. My father was the exact opposite. His anger and rage were so intense that he was often involved in bloody fights that worsened his heart problems.

Once we shed the feeling of being strangers, my older sister and I explored the area on our own. Day after day, we rushed from one tent to another, eagerly listening to the stories people told each other. Amidst the misery of famine, theft, and disease, there were also beautiful moments. Children were born, bringing hope with their cries amidst silent despair.

At our father's behest, we begged for a pen and a small piece of cardboard on which we wrote "Help" in capital letters. On the way back, we always walked along the fence, holding our sign outside for hours, hoping someone would rescue us. The guards weren't particularly pleased with our defiance, but they let us be, knowing there was no escape anyway. The longer we were locked up, the greater our desire for freedom became. My sister Samira was the rebel in our family and resembled my father more. He passed away on my tenth birthday, a year after our arrival.

That was the turning point that changed everything. From then on, my mother became a completely different person. She ingratiated herself with a soldier who fell blindly in love with her and informed her about the camp's weaknesses. She passed on this knowledge to us, asking us to seek help. We didn't know what was happening to us and were paralyzed by fear, which held us back for a long time. Nevertheless, we dared the breakout and climbed over the barbed wire fence into freedom in a night and fog operation. With a burning rage in my stomach, I ran towards the desert and abruptly stopped when I realized Samira wasn't by my side. Confused, I turned around and called out to my sister, who stood completely bewildered between me and the refugee camp. Our mother clung to its fence, shedding bitter tears. Convinced I would make it, I let her go back and struggled alone to the city.

Completely exhausted, I arrived early in the morning. Street children were everywhere, begging and fighting for survival. After my march, I was so weakened that I barely made it into a shop, where I collapsed while opening a bottle of water.

When I regained consciousness, the owner held out my described cardboard sign and asked what it meant. I was dazed and repeated my mother's name several times before stepping back again. Initially confused, he then put two and two together and knew exactly where I came from.

Five long days passed before I finally managed to get out of bed. The first thought was of my family, so the owner closed his shop before closing time and drove me back to the refugee camp. Although I kept talking incessantly, not a second passed without me thinking of my loved ones, whom I mentally embraced. On-site, I stayed in the car for the time being. With palpitations, I watched the shop owner talk to the soldier, who shrugged and pointed to his colleague, the admirer of my mother.

My longing grew immeasurable and suddenly became so great that I forgot everything around me and stormed straight to the fence. At the sight of me, his otherwise friendly expression changed, immediately letting me sense that something was wrong. For minutes, I questioned him in vain. Until he finally came out with the truth and, with a voice choked with tears, recounted the terrible events that had occurred two days earlier. He told how two young men attacked one of his comrades and seized his rifle. In their desperation, they demanded the immediate opening of the camp, which was refused. They then barricaded themselves with several people in one of the tents, among whom were my mother and my sister. Until the early hours of the morning, they repeated their demands in vain before executing their hostages and then themselves. At first, I didn't believe what he said. Only when our eyes met did I realize that from now on, I was alone in this world. Wailing, I collapsed and crouched on the ground for minutes. Then, I noticed beneath me the grass, carrying the scent and hope of the approaching spring.

Farewell without return

Although most of them had listened attentively to the story, Diyar was the only one brave enough to ask anything. Meanwhile, Amira and Zainab whispered to each other and looked interestedly over at Rubi, who nervously took a drag from his cigarette and abruptly interrupted the conversation.

»What are you actually staring at so curiously? Do you have any more questions? If so, you're too late because I have nothing more to say.« The women were so intimidated by his brusque tone that they eventually sent Bassem forward, who approached the helmsman.

»They just wanted to express their condolences. Nothing more. By the way, some of us are from the same region as you, which means a lot to them.«

»Really? That's great. Sorry, Diyar, but we'll have to postpone our conversation. Take over and always keep an eye on the...«

»The compass, I know. I know.«

»Thanks. It'll only take a moment.« For two whole hours, Rubi exchanged with his fellow sufferers. They conversed in their native language and shared their experiences, looking back on them with both tears and laughter. Afterwards, he seemed transformed and took over the helm with a smile.

»May I ask why you shine brighter than the sun itself?«

»By all means, but don't expect an answer. Don't look so surprised now, I'm just teasing you.«

»Thank goodness.« he said with relief.

»The reason for my good mood is due to the feeling of connection. It's great to speak with brothers and sisters who remind me of where my roots lie. In all the chaos around me, it's a welcome change. Help me remember, what were we talking about before?«

»Well, first about your dear father. But then, for some reason, you brought up Nabih.«

»Yes, exactly. I wanted to know why you're being so secretive about your friend's fate.«

»But I'm not.«

»Your eyes say something entirely different. So, if you want to enlighten us, now would be the ideal time, all eyes are on you.«

»Does it really have to be?«

»No one is going to force you. But there won't be too many more opportunities, as we're not far from our destination now.« Several seconds passed before Diyar gathered his courage and revealed the last part of the story.

»After we left the desert, the police took Nabih into custody again near his house. Thanks to my grandfather's good connections, they let us go. But the discomfort that the arrest caused me was immense, as I knew there was nothing more I could do for my best friend. The feeling of helplessness was only overshadowed by the war that had now reached the gates of our city.

Out of fear of attacks, checkpoints were hastily erected all over the city, which could only be passed after a body search. My crossing was only a few days away. Without my parents' knowledge, I gathered my meager belongings and went to the street children, whom I gifted with clothes and toys.

Afterwards, terrible self-doubt overcame me, so I ran the same way back, the one I used to walk with Nabih from school. I walked through the park and sat by the magnificent river, where, upon looking at the colorful flowers, I reviewed our conversations.

How I wished I could create imaginative castles in the air with him once more. Talked about our wishes and dreams that we exchanged during countless desert expeditions in the blazing heat. Piece by piece, this beautiful place will decay, and the only thing that will remain will be fragments that remind me of that time.

Lost in thought, I glanced at the family next to me, celebrating their son's birthday, which reminded me a bit of my own family. What will happen to them when I'm no longer here? Will they break in my absence, or will they even become victims of the war? All of this haunted my mind incessantly.

Soon after, I continued further into the city and realized that the smell I once associated with my childhood was no longer the same. Above all, there was suddenly fear. This even silenced the favorite melody of Monsieur Impeccable, the fruit vendor, who usually shared his philosophical anecdotes. On the way, I passed by the shop of old Friedrich, which was now closed and completely emptied. Only the inscription on the facade reminded me of the man to whom Nabih and I owed our lives.

As the evening door opened, I could hardly believe my eyes because the entire extended family had gathered to bid me farewell. Even those whom I hadn't seen in years due to a family feud.

Now I sat amidst these wonderful people, constantly pondering, which Bennou naturally noticed.

»If I didn't know better, I'd say you're thinking about something unsolvable, am I right?«

»You're close, Grandpa.«

»I'd be disappointed if I missed the mark, after all, you're my grandson.« he winked.

»Your keen mind doesn't miss anything either.«

»What troubles you? Is it because of Nabih?«

»It's just everything that's hitting me right now. But the question that's currently bothering me the most is this. Why did our entire family only come together at my departure? Don't get me wrong, it's really nice, but at the same time, it makes me endlessly sad. Because the time when we had no contact will never come back.«

»It's not just with us. That always happens when external circumstances become uncontrollable dimensions. Just think about the earthquake disaster last year, which cost tens of thousands of our neighbors their lives. Suddenly, all countries united and, regardless of their problems, worked together.«

»And before that, they let the weapons speak for years and didn't speak a word to each other.«

»Exactly, my boy, just with the difference that we chose the separation ourselves, and none of the politicians spoke on our behalf.«

»Yes, apparently.« Diyar added, disheart-ened.

»Now listen to me carefully. No matter how strong the external influences may be on you, don't let them cloud your judgment. Even if you don't realize it yet. Challenges will come your way that will loom like an insurmountable wall in front of you. These you will not conquer with your experience, but only with your heart.«

»Can you elaborate on that so that I can better prepare myself?« he replied with a serious expression.

»I wish I could. Every situation you face will be completely different from what I think I know. It's better if you just react when the time comes.«

»That doesn't sound very promising.«

»Don't give up before it even starts. Of course, nothing may happen. But with that naivety, I will never let you go.«

»Have you ever been in such a situation?«

»Of course!« Grandpa Bennou ran his hand through his beard.

»Please, let me share your thoughts. Perhaps it will be the last time we can talk about things like these.«

»To be honest, I don't think that's a very good idea.«

»Why?«

»You're already completely restless inside. I'm afraid that afterwards, you'll only exist out of fear and act accordingly.«

»Oh come on, give it a shot. Besides, you made it clear to old Friedrich that I'm tough. It can't be that bad.«

»Your persistence convinced me. But in return, you'll get me a coffee.« While the other family members engaged in lively conversation, the two sat in the other corner of the room, where Bennou delved into the past with a gentle tone. Before I walked under my magnificent date palms, I had to overcome many obstacles. I've told you about some, but I kept most of them to myself for a good reason. In my childhood, I earned my money on the bustling streets, where I sold homemade candies to locals and tourists alike. Some mistook me for an orphan, as I was the only kid wandering around in the urban jungle. I spent most sunsets by a lake surrounded by breathtaking mountains. Captivated, I watched several flamingos, who landed in the shallow water every evening. These beautiful moments, I deeply anchored in my subconscious, as my home life was anything but sheltered.

Baba was a brutal bully who spared neither me nor my mother. Whenever the desperate cries echoed at the end of the street, I built up an inner shield that deflected the desperate screams from my soul.

My personality was strong enough to withstand the beatings without psychological scars. However, my brother was the exact opposite and took every blow to heart. The resentment that had accumulated over the years became so overwhelming that I swore to leave. I repeatedly tried to persuade Hamza to join me, but he refused and clung desperately to our parents.

When Father got wind of my escape plans years later, he beat me so badly that he broke my nose. Bloodied, I ran away. Like a wretch, I crouched at my favorite spot, where I watched the rising wave movements of the floating ducks, which made it clear to me that I had to act quickly.

With a pounding heart, I sneaked into the house early in the morning and grabbed my savings. Just before I stepped out, Baba raised his hand threateningly. Unlike before, I didn't flinch, causing him to abandon his intention. He pursued me all the way up into the mountains. Then I turned decisively and faced him with a clenched fist. But what I saw wasn't the opponent I had hoped for, but only a stranger, numbed by alcohol, whom I once called father.

»Where will you go, my son?« came hesitantly from his mouth. I was completely perplexed because what he said touched me for some reason. Despite everything, I showed no emotions and replied briefly.

»Your addiction is your best friend. What happens to me has never interested you or Mum.«

»Can you forgive me someday?«

»Not after what you've done to us.«

»Please, try to understand, I...«

»I understand quite well. Leave me alone and try to be a good person for the rest of your life.« Bennou interrupted him. Silently, he withdrew until he disappeared from my life forever. My brother had to endure his tyranny for many years until he took his own life on his birthday. Mother, after Hamza's suicide, disowned him and married another man with whom she left the country. I never saw her again. And honestly, I never felt the need to, as the hatred I carried inside me was simply too great.

From then on, there was no turning back. Looking back, it was the best thing that could have happened to me. Since nobody beat me anymore, and I began to shape my future like a sculptor. At first, it drew me into the distance of the big city. There, I lived in an abandoned house where I encountered a wise old man named Malik, who, for inexplicable reasons, took me under his wing.

We talked for hours about life. Although, in my younger years, I was very interested in material goods, he quickly taught me that happiness is not found in lifeless things. Instead, it's much more about finding contentment in the silence of desirelessness. I didn't quite understand what he meant, and I argued from my limited knowledge. Then, he nudged me and pointed upwards with the following words:

»We humans structure our day according to the sun. But we will only understand the goodness of life in its entirety when the moon watches over us.«

After some time, I found work in an upscale suburb far removed from my own reality. With my makeshift cart, I roamed the streets, rummaged through containers, and collected trash that I sold in the evening. While doing so, I observed the people who secluded themselves from the outside world in their area, and I noticed, from their disdainful looks, that I would never be one of them. Poverty dramatically increased over the next few years, leading to greater and greater competition among the street children. This resulted in brutal turf wars where life and death were at stake.

One evening, as I rummaged through a container, I suddenly heard a faint whimpering. At first, I thought my mind was playing tricks on me. Then I dug deeper until I uncovered a face buried under garbage. I was completely shocked and pulled the little one, who had no strength, out. At the roadside, I cleaned his clothes of the horribly smelling food remnants and gave him water, which he drank in one gulp. After he had somewhat recovered, he told of his ordeal, which quickly turned from pity to blind rage.

Like me, he came from a broken family that abused him every day. Eventually, he made the decision to run away from home. On the streets, he found like-minded people who gave him work and took care of him. At night, he unknowingly stepped into the territory of a rival group while collecting garbage, and they brutally beat him before throwing him off a bridge. In excruciating pain, he dragged himself back to his zone, where he was discovered by me in a trash bin after over two days.

Without hesitation, I took him with me, which Malik wasn't particularly thrilled about at first. However, he quickly got used to the new roommate, who, at just five years old and with his boundless energy, turned our daily routine upside down. From that moment on, we were inseparable. I took Nael under my wing and roamed the streets with him. Although he was much younger, the circumstances in which he grew up quickly made him mature. This was evident in his profound thoughts, which repeatedly surfaced amidst his childish features.

Everything went smoothly until one day, we encountered the people in our territory who had thrown him off the bridge months earlier, like a lifeless piece of cattle. He immediately stood behind me, trembling, and clung to my shirt, peering out and whispering to me fearfully.

»It was the big one, the one with the blue pants.«

I asked again. Then I lunged at the guy, raining blows on him with an iron rod until he stopped moving. His friends were so intimidated by the action that they simply vanished and never showed their faces in our neighborhood again. Many years passed. During that time, Malik, who meant a lot to us as a father figure, passed away, although he found the idea terribly cheesy and vehemently rejected it. Nael had meanwhile matured into a young man and gradually emancipated himself from my care. On a spring day in May, it became clear to me that I had to say goodbye. Having fallen deeply in love a month prior, I wanted to provide my future wife a life away from poverty. In the circumstances I grew up in, it was understood by everyone that a farewell always meant a farewell without return. Although Nael was unaware of my plans, he sensed my changed behavior, which led him to wake me up in the middle of the night.

»Big brother, is it true that you're leaving?« At first, I beat around the bush and made excuses. But then, I felt such a guilty conscience that I ultimately came clean to him.

»I'm sorry for lying to you, but I have to bid you farewell.« Nael was completely distraught and stared into space for seconds.

»It's hard to cope with, and honestly, I'm not sure how to respond. Just the thought of not being able to stroll through the streets with you anymore takes away my ability to look forward to the next day.«

»I knew it would hit you hard, which is why I hesitated for so long. I would have preferred not to tell you at all. But that would have only increased my inner pain.«

»If it were up to me, I would freeze this moment forever. I detest farewells and everything that comes with them. Malik was right about what he once said, even though I didn't understand it back then.«

»What are you talking about?«

»Well, his two famous quotes that he recited to us while strolling through the bazaar.«

»You're funny. There were plenty of those.«

»I may have been young when I came to you, but I haven't forgotten that one.«

»I'm intrigued. And don't forget the appropriate tone, or it's completely unbelievable.«

»People who grow up in poverty usually die in poverty. The only thing…«

»The only thing they have in their lifetime is friends who become like family due to their solidarity.« Bennou finished the sentence with a smile.

»Yes, exactly.« Nael's eyes sparkled.

»Please, keep this in your heart. Even if thousands of kilometers separate us, you'll always be my little brother.«

»I will.«

»Now let's get some sleep, we have a long day ahead of us.« Several months later, I returned to the place where I grew up, not entirely willingly, as I was drafted into the army. Despite the constant threat from our neighbors, those were the most peaceful years of my life, during which I didn't fire a single shot. Looking back, I must admit that I was truly lucky and grateful to have been there at that time. I forged some friendships that lasted for many decades. One companion from those days passed away after a long illness. He was a funny joker and joked even then, when drunk, that I would live the longest because I treated my body and soul like a temple. Then came the war, which turned much of the country into rubble and ash. Although the extent in our region wasn't truly felt yet, I decided for safety reasons to evacuate my family to the neighboring country. At that time, I had just moved into my modest house, which I couldn't leave behind. Initially, I had sworn to never harm another person. However, that changed abruptly when I heard of the atrocities that had occurred in the neighboring village. In a covert operation, I gathered all my acquaintances and friends. Until the early hours of the morning, we dug three-meter-deep holes on the property, which we then prepared to remain invisible from the outside.

I knew that one day there would be a confrontation with the invaders, which is why a loaded handgun lay under my pillow. The tension escalated to immeasurable levels in the following weeks. Until one night, I heard several screams coming from outside into the bedroom. With the pistol in front of me, I rushed to the kitchen window and peeked out into the darkness behind the curtain. When I saw no one, I knew that my traps had been successful and went back to bed.

At sunrise, I cautiously stepped outside and checked the holes one by one, where I found four young soldiers desperately crying for help. When I responded in their native language, they looked up in surprise and begged for their release. However, I ignored their demands, exchanged weapons for water, and left them in the holes until their will was broken. One of them, however, was not to be deterred and swore revenge. In his grandiose speeches, he imagined killing me in a hundred different ways, which eventually even made his comrades laugh loudly, urging him to shut up. Three weeks later, our army regained control over the southern territories. At dawn, we pulled the intruders out of their holes, who were quite wobbly on their feet. At the sight of them, my inner tension discharged into a slap that landed loudly on the face of the hothead, who didn't know which way was up for minutes.

Since at that time it wasn't clear how to handle prisoners of war, I took advantage of the situation and sentenced the four of them to work. They renovated my house and planted hundreds of date palms, laying the foundation for my future earnings.

After just a few months, there was a tearful reunion with my family, who couldn't bear to stay abroad despite the ongoing war. Just as Bennou was about to take a breath, Diyar hastily interrupted, causing quite a bit of surprise.

»Grandpa, I think they released Nabih from prison?«

»You're quite impulsive. What makes you think that now?«

»Your whole life story just reminded me of him. I have a feeling.«

»And you must absolutely follow that feeling. Right?«

»Of course, but I don't know where to start looking?«

»First of all, I would visit his home. If he's not there, check the surrounding checkpoints. If anyone has seen him, it would be there.« Full of enthusiasm, Diyar jumped up and was about to disappear towards the exit when his grandpa grabbed his leg firmly.

»Here, take a photo with you. You know how people's memory is nowadays. They can't even remember their own names.« Twenty minutes later, Diyar arrived at his friend's parents' house. After receiving no response to his knocking, he moved further into the city, checking one checkpoint after another until dusk. Internally, he had already given up hope when someone directed him to a nearby address where he suspected his friend to be.

As he turned the corner, he could see Nabih in the distance, patrolling the street in military attire with a rifle over his shoulder. The initial contact between the two was distant. They talked, but Nabih had that infinite sadness in his eyes, the sadness that speaks of a broken heart.

»I can almost hear your thoughts, you look so downcast as you stare at me.«

»If you knew how much I've been looking forward to this moment. When did you get out of prison?«

»Two days ago.«

»Are you okay? You look tired.«

»No, not at all. It's no wonder, I've been guarding this sector for forty-eight hours straight, without sleep or food. When I finally rest, I have nightmares where terrible images haunt me.«

»What have they done to you?«

»What I endured during captivity, I somehow brushed off. But what I saw has changed me.« Motionless, Diyar looked into his friend's eyes, overwhelmed by immense feelings of guilt.

»Please don't cry. You can't blame yourself for what happened to me.«

»But…« he sobbed quietly.

»Why?«

»I could have done more. It wasn't enough.«

»It was more than I ever could have dreamed of. Because of me, old Friedrich had to die. Did you want to follow in his footsteps?«

»Don't talk like that, it makes me furious and the situation even more unbearable than it already is. Understand, it's not just me. We both deserve to get on that damn ship.«

»Life doesn't conform to our expectations, you should know that best.«

»I warn you, if necessary, I'll smuggle you onto the boat.«

»Be realistic. You'll be lucky if you reach it without any injuries. Many dangers lurk along the way, of which I was previously unaware.

Mines, snipers, and insurgents holed up in houses. Do you remember the explosion from last night?«

»Don't change the subject, I wasn't finished.«

»I'm deadly serious. Did you feel the shock?«

»Yes.«

»That wasn't a rocket strike as reported in the news. It was a suicide bomber who detonated himself at a checkpoint. I was only a hundred meters away and consider myself lucky to still be among the living. Do you understand the seriousness of the situation now?«

»I was already aware of that. But why are you so concerned? I'll manage somehow.«

»Somehow leads to the afterlife. But it's not a well-thought-out plan. Without me, you won't arrive unscathed, believe me.«

»Alright. Who knows, maybe a spot will open up and you can come with me?«

»Don't dream too much, we're not in a movie. When do you have to be at the port?«

»Two hours before midnight the day after tomorrow.« Suddenly, gunshots were heard in the distance, causing Nabih to nervously turn around and reach for his weapon.

»I'll be with you two hours before midnight the day after tomorrow.« As the gunfire resumed, he ran off and disappeared into the alleyways. All present held hands, eagerly anticipating the outcome of the story, while Rubi the helmsman inevitably steered towards the storm looming ahead of them.

War in Our Hearts

One day before my escape, in the afternoon, I visited Bennou again, who, despite the impending war, was taking a leisurely stroll through his date palm plantation. Numerous thoughts raced through my mind, manifesting as a suffocating feeling that had trapped me inwardly for days.

»Grandpa, how is it that I'm paralyzed with fear and you're so composed? Aren't you afraid of the war?«

»Every word has meaning. This meaning, you've adopted throughout your life. From your parents, friends, or from a dictionary. The question is, does the word trouble you or what it triggers within you?«

»I'm not entirely sure, I think I just react to

it.«

»Spoken words evoke emotions and create images. Images and emotions that make you happy or fearful. Correct?«

»Yes, I suppose so.«

»Are you truly aware of what I'm saying, or are you just responding to please me?«

»I'm trying to grasp it somehow.«

»Trying? Look at me. Do you remember what I recently told you about the war within our hearts?«

»I can recall a sentence or two.«

»Go ahead, I'm listening.«

»An external conflict always precedes an internal conflict. A small one within me or you doesn't have significant effects. But a conflict brewing within someone who holds authority and power can set off a fatal process, plunging the world into the abyss. All this, one should...« Diyar seemed to lose his train of thought.

»Let me step in before we stand here until tomorrow. Regardless of how big or small the conflict may be, you must analyze it with a clear mind. So that it dissolves through direct understanding and doesn't pile up into something significant that takes root and leads to a war within your heart.«

»Go on.«

»Wait, let me catch my breath first.«

»Forgive me, but I seem to have inherited impatience from Baba.«

»Listen! If you were to analyze the word 'war' with a clear mind, it would inevitably dissolve, thus not eliciting any emotions. However, because you approach it with a mind bound by experiences from the past, your emotions hold you captive, making it impossible for you to immediately dissolve this thought process.«

»Even if words no longer evoke emotions within me, war is still a reality, isn't it?«

»Yes, that's undeniable. But imagine if the war within our hearts didn't exist. Then, the word itself would ultimately be meaningless, as we would live in peace with each other. When you become aware of this, you view the world around you from a different perspective because you understand yourself better.«

»Now I understand why the word 'war' doesn't scare you as such. I hope I can say the same one day.«

»Even though it might sometimes seem from the outside that I'm tough and unfair, I'm not. But you must face life with a certain realism because it doesn't pause for ignorance. That's why it's of utmost urgency for you to absorb as much of my knowledge as possible. It doesn't mean you can simply adopt my way of thinking. However, it's a nudge in the right direction that speeds things up a bit.« Diyar agreed and followed Bennou to the end of the date palm plantation, where they settled down next to a felled tree.

»Look, this beautiful piece of nature was over three hundred years old.«

»How do you know that, did it speak to you?«

»I wish it did. You can tell from the individual rings when you count from the inside out.«

»That sounds a bit like life itself. Why was it cut down?«

»Everything on this Earth has its time. It was old and with its diseased roots, it would have infected the palm trees standing over there. Every attempt to save it was in vain. It affected me deeply because it was a loyal companion that gave me comfort in the darkest moments.« Bennou said, bidding farewell with a final touch. Soon after, he brought up Nabih, interrupting his grandson's thoughts.

»Sorry, I was so engrossed in our conversation that I completely forgot to ask you about your friend. I know from your father that he's out of prison, but he didn't mention how your reunion went.«

»I must admit, it didn't go as I had hoped.« Diyar sighed heavily.

»What do you mean?«

»When we met, he had this infinite sadness

in his eyes. That kind of sadness that's hard to describe in words, as you've never experienced it yourself. He was dressed in dark green military clothing and kept his hand on his weapon constantly. I don't know what they did to him, but I wish I could turn back time because to me, he's not the same anymore.«

»Stop blaming yourself for things you have no control over. You're facing the greatest challenge of your life, and you need a clear head. Do you think your friend would handle it differently if he were in your situation?«

»I honestly don't know what to believe at the moment. Tomorrow, an hour before midnight, Nabih will pick me up. How will I survive when everything around me feels like an endless nightmare?«

»You're currently seeing everything around you through a veil of fear. That's why it's almost impossible for you to muster your inner strength. Are you sure you don't want anyone from your family to accompany you?«

»No way, it's way too dangerous. Besides, I could never bear to see you or Baba cry. I hope you're not upset and respect my decision.« Nodding, Bennou reached into his pocket and handed his grandson a thick bundle of banknotes, which he held uncertainly in his hands.

»That's a fortune. I can't possibly accept this.«

»Perhaps with us. In Europe, this robber's currency is worthless. Take it already. I can't do anything with this lifeless paper. I can't eat it, and if I plant it, it won't grow into a tree. Come on, get going slowly so your family still has something of you. I'll come by tomorrow at sunset.« The next evening, Diyar was completely on edge. He kept checking the time and looking out the window, hoping to catch a glimpse of his grandpa, but in vain. Nabih was punctual to the minute and silently witnessed the tearful farewell, right in front of the house. Soon after, he urged Diyar to hurry. But Diyar stubbornly refused to leave his parents and begged until his friend finally pulled him away.

»Come on, we can't wait forever.«

»But what about Bennou?« he spoke in desperation.

»Bennou will understand. Grab your bag and let's go.« Diyar glanced back multiple times. Then he gave his loved ones one last kiss and followed his friend, who briskly headed towards the harbor.

»Hey, why are you running? Couldn't we have waited a moment longer? After all, Grandpa promised he'd come by.«

»No, there's no time for that. We're already late.« Nabih said urgently, pointing to his wristwatch.

»What happened to the gentle guy I once searched for artifacts within the desert?«

»He's still within me. He just temporarily exchanged his shovel for a weapon.« he chuckled loudly.

»Do you have a plan for getting safely to the harbor? Or are you still relying on your intuition like before?«

»If I did that, I'd be six feet under by now. Our adversaries are always on the move. Yesterday, they holed up in that house over there.

Today, they're somewhere else already, that's what makes it so dangerous, you never know if death is lurking around the next corner. Come this way.«

»Wait, I don't have a good feeling about this. That dark corner seems perfect for an ambush.« Just as Nabih was about to reply, two armed men jumped out of hiding onto the street, gunning down everyone in the immediate vicinity. Pale with fear, Diyar crouched behind a parked car, while his friend took out the attackers with two precise shots.

»Move, we need to keep going.« Wordlessly, he followed his friend, who kept talking to him while the horrific images seared into his mind.

»Don't you feel guilty about what you just did?«

»No one forced those lunatics to stage such a circus and murder innocents. Look at it this way. If I hadn't acted, we'd be the ones being scraped off the pavement.« he said casually.

»From the way you're talking, it sounds like you couldn't care less that those two are no longer alive.«

»It's time for you to wake up slowly. The harsh reality of war doesn't seem to have reached you yet.«

»Do you think so?«

»Yes, of course. Otherwise, you wouldn't have asked me such weird questions. Just seeing a few enemy rockets flying over your head doesn't tell you anything.«

»For me, that's more than enough. I don't need to see people losing their lives to understand that war is nothing good.«

»Don't stare at me like that, my friend, I'm just teasing you. I'd prefer not to have seen all this either. But, I have to come to terms with it. Do you see the smoke plumes back there?«

»Yes. You know what that reminds me of?«

»The war. What else?«

»No, no. It reminds me of what your mother once said. The smell carried by those dark plumes of smoke isn't just any scent. It's the scent of a burnt future. Our future.«

»Sure, now that you mention it.«

»Yes, but before, I didn't really understand that. But today, everything seems to be in a different light.«

»I immediately grasped what that means for our generation, even if I didn't want to admit it. War is something so cruel that defies all logic. That's probably why people only realize it when it's too late.« After an hour, they reached a hill from where they could see the dark sea, which filled Diyar with growing unease.

»From here, it's not far anymore. In close proximity, within the ruins, sharpshooters are most likely lurking. So, I suggest we cautiously move through the minefield.«

»That doesn't sound like a good idea.«

»Don't worry. Most of them are deactivated.«

»And what about the others?«

»Well, those are active and still buried somewhere underground. You can tell by the warning sign with the skull.«

»Are you kidding me?«

»Not at all, but sacrificing a leg is still better than being executed with a headshot.«

»Well, I find both options terrible.«

»If you don't have a better idea, I'd suggest you stick close to my heels but at a safe distance.«

»Do you at least have a flashlight so I know where I'm stepping?«

»A flashlight? All we need is a good dose of luck and my machine gun to pave the way to freedom.« With a sinking feeling in his bones, he followed his friend down to the minefield, where they weren't the only ones.

»Should we let the others go first or should we take the lead?« Diyar nervously bit his nails.

»Look at the uncertain faces. They've also thought of that idea. I think if we don't go first, you'll miss your passage.«

»That's not going to help me at all if we're

the first ones to meet our end.« Without much thought, Nabih started walking, carefully considering every step. Three meters behind him, his friend followed, beads of cold sweat forming on his forehead. When he heard voices, he urged the people behind him to be cautious. However, they were so preoccupied that no one paid attention to him. Shortly after, a loud click was heard, prompting Diyar to shout at a woman carrying her child to stop. Nabih swiftly ran back and gradually uncovered the mine that seemed ready to explode at any moment. Around them, the desperation of the people facing the seemingly hopeless situation was evident as they prayed. Fortunately, he soon confirmed that it was a disarmed mine. With a sigh of relief, they continued toward the port. In the background, one could hear skirmishes that, upon closer listening, were getting closer.

»Nabih, what was that?« he called out to his friend, bewildered.

»No idea. Probably our army taking out a few poor souls.« Nabih replied.

»Are you sure?«

»No, but if you keep bombarding me with questions, I can't see where I'm stepping.«

»Then look ahead, damn it.«

»I am, but in this darkness, every step could be your last.« Meanwhile, one of the enemy snipers had stealthily approached the mine-field and started firing at anything in sight. Panic ensued, causing everyone to stray from the original path, triggering one explosion after another. Diyar instinctively grabbed the child and ran with the woman in tow, following his friend, who found a way out of the hellish situation in the cover of darkness. From a safe distance, they could vaguely make out the bodies on the dusty ground, lives lost unnecessarily. Ten minutes later, they safely reached the port, where chaotic scenes unfolded. People were running around, desperately seeking passage to escape the war.

»Where does your boat depart from?« Nabih squeezed through a throng of people.

»How am I supposed to know? I don't have a ticket!« he called out, feeling lost.

»They must recognize you somehow.«

»All I know is that I'm on a list, nothing more.«

»Well, then let's ask around. We don't have much time left.« Suddenly, Bennou appeared out of nowhere. He stood amidst the chaos, pointing toward the blue-painted boat that would soon carry his grandson to freedom. As the two embraced, shedding tears, Nabih was overwhelmed by a flood of emotions, wiping away a tear or two unnoticed. Suddenly, nearby enemy rockets struck, causing a sudden shift in mood. This led some refugees to miss their departure, as the smugglers threw their original departure times into disarray. Diyar's boat was one of the last to prepare for departure. Just before he boarded, he hugged his friend, slipping some money to him and entrusting him with these words:

»Do you know what reassures me?«

»No.« his friend replied, visibly downtrodden.

»We're not the only ones on this beautiful

Earth separating from each other. Out there, millions are leaving their homes, going through what we're experiencing. Each of these stories is unique. Ours, filled with adventures, hope, and courage. It won't outlast us. But our dreams will.« Fully loaded, we set sail, heading out onto the open sea, where an endless melancholy enveloped my thoughts. It can't be true, I keep telling myself that this is all just a dream. Frightened, I stare at the ground, and with every wave crashing against the hull of our boat on this starry night, I realize that I've left behind the most precious thing in the world.

Silence of Solitude

The first to speak after the story was Bassem. He sat tense, observing others who didn't exchange a word, bravely enduring the uncontrollable waves.

»Young man, I have no clue if we'll survive. But I wanted you to know that you deserve your place on this boat just like anyone else. At first, I didn't like you. But only because you resembled my own sons, whose hearts were as big as yours.«
Diyar responded to the address with a smile and was immediately embraced by little Adil, whose mother also held onto him.

»My son feels safest with you. He would never approach someone he didn't fully trust. At the start of our escape, I thought our journey would be a piece of cake. But now, looking at the sky and the sea, I feel like the world is about to crash upon us.«

Internally, Diyar was also overwhelmed by fear, reminding him.

»Challenges will come before you like an insurmountable wall. You won't conquer them with your experience, only with your heart.« As Diyar was called over by Rubi, he staggered toward them, clutching onto his fellow travelers, whose fear was evident in their eyes.

»I have bad news. We probably won't make it to the destination.« shouted the helmsman, his face whipped by the spray.

»Are you sure? How far do we have left?«

»We're relatively close. The waves are holding us back so much that we're literally standing still. If the weather doesn't ease up, we'll run out of fuel in less than half an hour.«

»Then just turn off the engine and wait for the sea to calm down.« Diyar suggested, gripping the railing tightly.

»If I do that, we're at the mercy of the forces of nature. Go, inform the others and tell them it could get very dangerous.« Before he could run back, a breaker hit the boat from the side, and Adil fell overboard. Without hesitation, Diyar leaped into the waves and grabbed the boy, who was being dragged underwater by the strong current. Rubi immediately slowed down, turned on the searchlight, and circled around them. Everyone joined the rescue effort and finally managed, on the fourth attempt, to pull the little one back on board. Every attempt to save Diyar failed due to the strong waves, which kept pushing him away from his helpers. Over ten times, they tried, until Rubi reluctantly gave up and turned away. Despite the storm, I could hear voices calling out for me for minutes. Eventually, I was so exhausted that I just let myself drift and accepted the silence of solitude. The word "death" gradually crept into my thoughts. But instead of reacting from my experience, I analyzed it with a clear mind, freeing myself from the images and emotions I had carried throughout my life.

At dawn, my fellow sufferers arrived unharmed at their destination. Bassem, who lost his sons and wife due to a bitter war, disembarked first. Following him, little Adil and Zainab, who in an act of desperation prevented a totalitarian regime from building an atomic bomb. Abdul, the confused half-naked man, climbed over the railing. Then came Amira, who told the story of the fisherman Ibrahim and his friend Omar, who, due to his feelings of guilt, took his own life on the evening of his tragedy. Rubi bid farewell to the last refugees with a hug. Gazing at the sunrise, he thought wistfully of me and his family, who were once expelled and uprooted due to their ethnic minority. A day later, my lifeless body washed ashore. My journey didn't end here, it ended many years before, where someone carried war in their heart, and I had my future ahead of me.

»My name was Diyar.
Diyar means homeland.«

*For all those whose journey ended far too soon.
Who lost their lives in a war that once began
within.*

You enjoyed the book?

I'm truly glad you've read my book this far! If you enjoyed it, I'd really appreciate it if you left a review on the platform where you purchased the book. You can also share your thoughts on one of your favorite book review websites.

Your feedback is not only valuable to me, but it also helps support my work in writing more stories and reaching new readers.